The Convention

Inspired by True Events

by

Jeff T. Travis

authorHOUSE

1663 LIBERTY DRIVE, SUITE 200
BLOOMINGTON, INDIANA 47403
(800) 839-8640
www.authorhouse.com

This book is a work of fiction. Places, events, and situations in this story are purely fictional and any resemblance to actual persons, living or dead, is coincidental.

© 2004 Jeff T. Travis
All Rights Reserved.

No part of this book may be reproduced, stored in a retrieval system, or transmitted by any means without the written permission of the author.

First published by AuthorHouse 04/05/04

ISBN: 1-4184-1506-5 (e)
ISBN: 1-4184-1505-7 (sc)

Printed in the United States of America
Bloomington, Indiana

This book is printed on acid-free paper.

Special thanks to family and friends for taking time to read the original manuscript. I know how precious time is these days and appreciate your willingness to spend some of yours for me.

Table of Contents

CHAPTER ONE – SLEEP 1

CHAPTER TWO – THE STAIRWELL 6

CHAPTER THREE – THE BOULDER 23

CHAPTER FOUR – THE HITCHHIKER 56

CHAPTER FIVE – THE EMBRACE 72

CHAPTER SIX – THE PILLARS 97

CHAPTER SEVEN – THE PAINTINGS 107

CHAPTER EIGHT - MICHAEL'S FATHER SPEAKS 126

CHAPTER NINE – THE DECISION 152

CHAPTER ONE – SLEEP

"Hello"

"Hey, it's me."

"Oh hey sweetie, everything okay?"

"Oh yea, fine. I just called to chat a minute and check in. Everything okay with you and the boys?"

"Yea, everything's fine - - I was just getting ready to start the morning wake up ritual," she said with a little laugh. "You know, at least in that respect the boys are more like me than they are you."

"I'll give ya that one, not exactly morning people, are they?" Michael said with a voice lowering in pitch with each word spoken.

"Michael are you okay, you're sounding a little down this morning?"

"Oh no, no, I'm fine. I was sitting here missing you and the boys, so I thought I'd give you a call."

Knowing Michael and knowing he wasn't being truthful with her "you know, that's exactly why I married and love you Michael. I could tell when we were dating that was the type of person you were and would always be," she stated with her ever present loving and convincing tone.

"What type is that?"

"Loving and caring, sweetheart. Are you sure everything is okay? You're not feeling down on yourself again, are you?"

"I don't think so, but if I was, you got me over it - - just like you always do. How did I get so lucky to find you?"

"You are lucky mister and don't you forget it," she said jokingly.

"You laugh, but it's true! You are one awesome lady and there's no way I could ever forget it."

"Well look here, your oldest son just made his way in here all by himself. Good morning sweetie, did you sleep good? Honey, let me get off here so I can start my day."

"Okay, give the boys a big hug and kiss for me Lynn. I'm going to stretch out for a little while, I got woke up a couple of times last night."

"Did you get enough sleep? I don't want you working if your mind isn't sharp."

"Oh yea, I'm fine."

"I mean it Michael, I know you love your job, but it isn't worth it."

"I know, I know. I promise I got plenty of sleep. I'm just going to stretch out for a while. I'll let ya' go, don't forget to tell the boys I love 'em."

"Okay, I will. Love you."

"Love you too. Bye."

"Okay hot stuff, I'll see you tonight," she said in a sensual manner.

"Okay sweet stuff, see ya' tonight," he responded in a 'I'm ready now' tone to his voice.

Michael hung up the receiver and looked over at the clock. "5:50! Man, I shouldn't have called her this early," he thought as he stretched out on the couch. While laying there in his favorite "Worlds Greatest Dad" t-shirt, he thought just how lucky he was - - a beautiful wife and three

The Convention

wonderful sons who he loved more than life itself and would give anything, anything for - - including his own life.

"I'm sure I love them with every part of my heart and soul and I know that they love me" - - still he felt something was missing as he thought to himself. "What am I not doing? Why don't I feel like a father, a good father, like my father? Am I trying to live up to something that I have no idea how to live up to? Why was it so easy for my father to do everything right while I was growing up?" Soon, Michael gave out several yawns - - "man, I am exhausted," he thought. With that, Michael stretched his left arm up and covered his eyes with his forearm and fell fast asleep.

CHAPTER TWO – THE STAIRWELL

"So many steps - - I sure wish I would have left this backpack behind now," Michael thought as he continued up the rear stairwell. Breathing heavier and heavier, he noticed that he was tiring more and more with each step he took. "I shouldn't be getting this tired, I'm stronger than this," he thought to himself. "This is much better than before though," reflecting back about a year, he remembered when he used to get tired just walking from the driveway to the house before losing the extra 70 pounds. "Now I'm 6' 2" and 205 pounds. I'm healthy, and I'm strong! No! I won't let these stairs beat me. In fact, I'm going to add climbing stairs to my exercise routine. You can't beat me."

The Convention

"What's that?" Michael said to himself. He could hear what he thought might be a voice crying out. He stopped for a moment so he could hear more clearly. Though he couldn't hear what was being said, he was certain this was the voice of someone needing help. Michael always prided himself on helping others. As if a light switch had been tripped, he was not tired anymore and was no longer breathing heavy. Letting go of the handrail to hold his backpack with both hands, he switched into high gear and began running up the steps - two and three at a time. Turning at the stair landing, he lost his footing and slammed into the wall, busting the knuckles on his left hand. He immediately and instinctively grabbed his left hand and began squeezing it with his right.

"Man was that stupid, I'm glad my brothers weren't here to see that - - I'd never hear the end of it," Michael said to himself while shaking his hand rapidly back and forth. He looked at his hand knowing that it must be banged up pretty good because it hurt so bad, and because he could feel blood dripping from it. "Well if there was better lighting in here, I might be able to tell how bad this cut is." Setting his backpack down, Michael unlatched the top portion and felt around on the inside for something to wrap around his hand. He pulled out a piece of cloth of some sort. "Well, I don't know exactly what this is, but it's going to have to work." Michael folded the end over a couple of times and placed that part over where he felt like the cut was. After doing so, he wrapped the remainder of the cloth around his hand three times and stuffed the end between his palm and the cloth to secure it.

Michael could hear the voice again. He didn't bother latching the top of his backpack. He stood up, threw the pack over his shoulder and started for the stairs. "Ouch! I must be the stupidest person alive," Michael said as his left hand slammed against the hand rail. Again, he instinctively grabbed and squeezed his hand. He could tell that the second injury hadn't helped matters any, as the cloth was already saturated with blood. Again the voice could be heard, but not made out. Michael continued holding pressure on his hand and pressed forward up the stairs.

"Ahhhhhhhhhhmaaaaaaaziiiiiiiiing Graaaaace, Hooooooow Sweeeeet the sound - thaaaat saaaved ahhhhha wretch liiiiiiike meeeeeeeeee, leeeeh ooooonce waaas lost, buuuut nowww amm found, waaaaas blind buuuuut nowww…

"Well hello there," Michael said.

"Oh my goodness, you startled me!" she said while sitting in the corner of the stairwell.

"I'm sorry. I could hear you while I was downstairs and thought you needed help. No offense, but it sounded like you were crying out until I got to the stairs just below you."

"No offense taken young man. I've never had the best singing voice, but I do love to sing, and I do love that song. I was singing to take my mind off the pain in my leg."

"Oh, you are hurt! Are you alright – do you need some help?"

"I don't think I can walk. The lights went out and I couldn't see where I was going. I tripped over something and lost my footing. My leg is hurting a little, but it's not so bad while it's stretched out here on the floor and I'm able to lean against the wall. I tried to stand up a little while ago. It hurt pretty bad, so I figured the best thing to do would be to sit back and relax. I'm not real sure, but I think it may be broken. When I fell, I went slightly to the side. That made my leg twist up under me - - I can't be sure, it happened so fast, but I think I heard it snap."

"I can certainly understand that," Michael said trying to catch his breath. "It's pretty dark in here," he said while glancing around. "About all I can make out at any distance are steps here and there and those darkened lines traveling up the stairs, that we both know are handrails. You know, come to think of it, it's not quite as dark right here, as it is down the stairs. There must be some light further up that's reflecting here."

"Yes, I agree. Just above us there's an exit sign lit up with a little dim light beside it. It's been flickering on and off for a couple of minutes. As for the handrail, the time that I've been sitting here, I've been pounding myself for not holding on to it while going down those steps. If I would have, I'd more than likely be on my feet instead of my butt right now."

"Yea" Michael said with a polite laugh. "Well, these things happen to the best of us - let me see if I can help you."

"What's that on your hand?" she inquired with concern.

"Oh, that's just a little bandage I fashioned out of a piece of cloth."

"You've cut your hand I take it - - is it a bad cut?"

"Oh no, I don't think so. It was bleeding a little, so I figured I'd better bandage it up," Michael commented nonchalantly, while knowing he had done a pretty good number on it.

"You know, as much blood as there is on that bandage, I'd say it's more of a cut than you think it is. Before you check my leg, why don't you let me check your hand? I'm pretty good at dealing with injuries when they're not my own."

"I really appreciate that, but I don't think it's necessary," he said. "Besides, I can tell that it has already stopped bleeding. Trust me, it was dripping a minute ago - - I couldn't see the blood, but I could feel it - - you know what I mean?"

"I certainly do young man, I certainly do. Aren't we a pair, a busted hand and a busted leg. Now, you quit trying to be my knight in shining armor for a minute and let me see your hand!"

"Really, it's…"

"I don't want to hear it! If you don't let me help you, you can just head on your way young man," she said with a commanding voice and determination in her eyes.

Realizing that she was not going to budge on her request, Michael pulled the tail of the makeshift bandage from the inside of his palm, twirled it around his right index finger and unraveled it, exposing the cut. When the last portion of the bandage was removed, it was obvious in the limited light that there must have been a jagged metal edge of some sort that his hand had impacted. This cut was massive, stretching from the top knuckle of his middle finger and traveling just beyond his wrist. It was a gaping wound that easily went to the bone for well over two inches, blood was literally pouring from it.

"You see, I was right. Now let me work my magic. Give me your hand," the woman said extending her hand out to meet his.

Michael submitted to her request. When he did, she placed one hand on his forearm and the other just above the wound. She began squeezing gently, but at the same time, very firmly.

"How did you do this young man?"

"Oh, I was walking up the stairs, and I guess there must have been a piece of metal or something attached to the wall above the handrail - - my hand must have slid under it or something."

"Well, my vote would be for the 'or something' part of that little story. You fell and hit something didn't you?"

"How did you know that?" Michael asked in a puzzled voice.

"Well, someone 'walking up' the steps hitting their hand like that, would have felt it long before it did that much damage because of their slowed pace. The way you were out of breath when I first saw you, it was pretty obvious to me that you were coming up those steps with everything you had."

After she finished explaining her version of the facts surrounding the accident to Michael, she let go of his arm and removed the scarf from around her neck, and began pulling the shoulder pad loose from the underside of her dress.

"Hold on a minute, don't tear your dress up!" Michael said with alarm and concern.

"Oh nonsense! Now reach your hand back over here before you get it to bleeding again."

"It's not bleeding! Heck, it's not even hurting anymore, you have some real talent!" Michael said with amazement.

"I told you young man, I'm very good with injuries that are within my reach and are not my own." She squeezed the wound together with one hand, and placed the shoulder pad into position with the other. "Well look there, the shoulder pad is the perfect size. Now you help hold the pad while I wrap this scarf around it." She completed two wraps and started removing the pad from the other side of her dress. As she did, Michael shook his head in disagreement with her actions.

"You don't approve, I sense?" she said lifting her eyebrows inquisitively.

"Well, I just don't like it that you've now torn up the other side of your dress for this."

"Young man, do you really think I could have worn this dress with a single shoulder pad? I would have looked like the hunchback of Notre Dame - - don't you think?"

Michael laughed and agreed.

Taking the other shoulder pad, she placed it between the scarf and his hand where she had stopped and then finished wrapping the wound. She slid the end of the scarf on the underside of his hand, starting at the wrist region and pushed it completely through the other side. She pulled it to form a tail and made the beginnings of a knot where she had started the tail.

"Okay now this is going to hurt for a second," she said looking to him for approval with warning. His eyes indicted that it would be fine.

She pulled it just beyond snug and was finished. "Now, isn't that much better?"

"No doubt about it, I can't feel any pain. In fact, if I didn't know I had cut it, I wouldn't think it was injured at all. I sure appreciate it."

"It's no bother young man, no bother at all," she said with a calming voice and gentle smile.

"Okay, my turn. Can I check your leg now?"

"That'll be fine, just fine. Just make sure you don't re-injure your hand."

Michael shook his head and let out a little snicker. He began checking her leg, starting near the ankle. While doing so, he got a feeling that she was not entirely comfortable. He couldn't quite pinpoint what the issue was, he could just tell. Something told him that he needed to talk to her - - that just talking to her would assure her that everything would be fine.

"Well, I've known you for two or three minutes now without knowing your name," Michael said with a befriending expression.

"Oh, I'm sorry," revealing a pleasant smile. "I guess we were both a little preoccupied. My name is Lilly - - Lilly Corning. And you, young man?" while reaching her hand out for his.

"Name's Michael. Very pleased to meet you Mrs. Corning. About how long have you been sitting here?"

"Not long at all, I was only able to sing my favorite song three or four times. Is it a favorite of yours Michael?"

"I'd say it's one of my favorites for that type of music. To be honest with you though, I'm a little more partial to classic rock and soft rock. It just gives me a 'pick-me-up'. You know what I mean?"

"I surely do Michael. It's nice to have music to fall back on when you're feeling depressed."

"Exactly! You hit the nail on the head. What do you do for a living Mrs. Corning?"

"I work in people relations here in the building, been working here for nearly twenty five years."

"Twenty five years, no way.! You're not old enough to have worked anywhere for twenty five years."

"Ohhh... ha hah,' she laughed. 'Oh, aren't you the flatterer. That's so very kind of you Michael, so very kind."

Michael could see all the beginning signs of an older person with Mrs. Corning, from her mannerisms, to her tender and warming voice, to the pronounced crows feet around her eyes and wrinkles on her cheeks. Michael thought to himself that she was probably sixty years old.

"If you don't mind my asking Mrs. Corning, how old are you?"

"You know, that's not the best way to get on the good side of a woman," she said with a polite wink of the eye and an accompanying pristine smile.

"I'm sorry Mrs. Corning," he said while thinking how unbelievably stupid the question was. "I was just trying to make conversation while I checked your leg. Please, forget I asked."

"Oh - - that's alright, perfectly alright. I really don't mind the question at all. Let's just say I'm much younger than I look, and far older than you really think I am."

Much younger than she looks and far older than I think she is, Michael repeated back to himself - - that makes no sense. I think she may be a little more shaken than she is letting on.

"You know, I used to be quite the looker in my days. My hair was so long and pretty, so pretty. I don't mind telling you Michael, I had a pretty good figure too. Ha hah. You know, my girlfriends used to say they'd kill for hair like mine. Oh, that was many years ago though, now I'm this lovely shade of silver - - cut short to represent my age and make it a little more manageable. But you know, it really doesn't bother me that I'm aged because I know that I'm also aging."

The Convention

"You're certainly right Mrs. Corning, it shouldn't bother you. My father has always told me that the 'more matured population,' that's the words he uses, pass down their wisdom so we can limit our mistakes." Not ignoring her confusing statement this time so he could get a better understanding as to her condition, "what do you mean when you say 'aged and aging' though?"

"Michael, it is so interesting that you would tell me what you just did. You see, being aged is a sign of ones journey through life, and aging is wisdom picked up along the way. Getting older really is perfectly fine Michael, getting old... now that's what will get you and those that love you. When you get old, you just seem to stop picking up wisdom. Or far worse, you stop passing it on to those who can use it. As long as a person continues to pass their wisdom on, they're really not getting older, they're simply aging, and while aging - - are getting closer to realizing all the important points of life - - and it's not being young Michael, it's being young in your heart."

"I like the way you put that Mrs. Corning – I think it explains getting older, or excuse me, maturing, very well. You just confirmed what my father has told me all along. I appreciate you sharing that with me. I need to remember the way you put it - - I really like it. Thanks."

"I learned that many years ago Michael, when I got this necklace. Can you see the three 'A's,?" she said while holding the chain and shifting it from side to side to get it to catch the little bit of light available. "It was given to me by my father," she said as her eyes opened fully capturing the intenseness of her smile.

"Yes, I do. Three 'A's'. Aged And Aging?

"You got it Michael," she said with a subtle nod of her head. I was twenty four years of age the day he gave it to me. It was a welcome home gift. My goodness, I remember I was so frightened that day," she said with her smile leaving her face and her head tilting slightly towards the ground.

"A welcome home gift and you were afraid? What were you frightened about?"

CHAPTER THREE – THE BOULDER

"Do you really want to know Michael - - it's not the most pleasant of stories?"

"If you don't mind telling me, I don't mind listening. I've heard my share of unpleasant stories," Michael said having sensed that she wanted to share it with him.

"Well, when I was twenty three years old I made the decision. I wanted to do something to help people less fortunate than myself. I, along with my dear husband and a few others from my church, went to Africa on a missionary trip. Oh Michael, those poor innocent children, it just broke my heart to see them and at the same time, completely filled my heart with overwhelming joy to know that I was given a chance to actually make a difference. It wasn't long before I knew we were making a difference too. Any person could tell by the way their eyes would light up when our monthly supplies would arrive. We were able to help them with food, clothing, blankets, bandages, medicines, education… you know… all the essentials. Sometimes we would even put some goodies in with the supplies. Some of these children were as much as fifteen years old Michael, and had never knew such a thing as candy even existed."

"Well, I was there for nearly one year, one year of my life that I wouldn't consider changing even one moment. I woke early one morning and decided I would make my way down to the stream to fill a container with water. It was quite a distance and the children had a bit of a tough time carrying that heavy water container."

"It was such a beautiful day, I remember it like it was yesterday. It was the bluest sky, just full of beautiful snow white clouds, and the sun was just beginning to break over the horizon. I was overcome with the moment and decided I would take a little walk along the stream. I walked for about a quarter mile, just enjoying the view and the crispness of the air. Right along the bank, about fifty yards off the path where I was walking, sat a huge boulder maybe fifteen feet above the water. It offered the perfect view and had a recess along the top that I thought would provide excellent seating."

"I made my way over there by pushing the branches and weeds out of my way, using a small stick I had picked up along the path. I reached the boulder, and using a tree to support myself, I climbed up and made myself comfortable in the crevice."

"Looking out onto the stream was just so beautiful Michael. The birds were singing and off in the distance was a family of monkeys playing in the branches. I could see water droplets caused by the dew falling from the branches as they would leap from limb to limb. I just sat there counting my blessings and reflecting on how the lives of the children had changed since our arrival, it truly was quite a dramatic change Michael. Small children are so incredibly honest. When children smile, you just know that what you're doing is right and good."

"All of the sudden, I heard a crunching and crackling sound from over my right shoulder. I turned my head and could see a tree limb on its way directly toward me! There was no time to get out of the path of it, all I had time to do was lean my body over and cover my head. It really happened so fast, I didn't even feel the impact."

"There I was pinned in the crevice of this boulder, with the tree limb stretched diagonally across my chest, waist and right side of my pelvis. Because I was in the crevice, I wasn't completely crushed by the limb, thank goodness. But at the same time, it was so very heavy there was no way I could move. I tried many, many times, I simply couldn't. I tried hollering for help, but that didn't work out well either. The weight of the limb just wouldn't allow me to scream out. It was then, that I realized that all I could do was pray to the good Lord for help - - and pray I did!"

"Well, I was getting some relief from the sun because of the leaves dangling above me, but the sun soon became very hot - - baking hot. I tried shifting my body little by little to get some of the pressure off of me, but it didn't work. I'll tell you, I was wedged in there so perfectly. A little less and I felt like I would be able to scream my lungs out. A little more and I would not have been able to breath. Of course, I was certain I would hear people from the village looking for me. That eased my worries for a good while, but I didn't hear anyone all day and soon the day turned to night."

"Oh, what a relief the night was from that searing heat! At least until I heard animals beginning to make their way about. Are you sure you want to hear this Michael?"

"Are you kidding me? There's no way you're not finishing this story! I'm afraid that I already know what you're going to say," Michael said with fear in his voice.

"Well, the limb is across my chest, and my arms are above the limb. Because the limb was diagonal across me, I was able to move my left arm far more than my right. Neither could be moved very much though. For about the next hour, I continued to hear animals walking through brush. At times, just because of how much noise there was with the brush, I began to pick up on the varying sizes - - most I could tell were quite small."

"I heard what I thought was clawing on the tree that I had used to make my way onto the boulder. I looked over to my right as much as I could and saw it come into view. Sure enough, I was right - - an animal had found me! I don't know for sure just what kind of animal it was, but I wasn't taking any chances. It came into reach of my right arm and I swatted it across the chest and leg, knocking it off the boulder. It squealed when I hit it and I heard it impact the ground. It was a pretty good fall for it, but it wasn't hurt in the least - - I heard it wander off into the brush. I was happy that I hadn't harmed it. I mean that wasn't my intention. I just didn't want it around me."

"Unfortunately however, the animal returned and this time he brought some of his family members with him. When they would come up around my face, I could swat at them so that wasn't so bad. What was tough was my lower body. They had figured out a way to climb the boulder from the stream side. I couldn't see them coming, and even if I could, I couldn't swat at them because of the size of the limb - - my arms couldn't reach over it."

The Convention

"Michael, the feeling of them crawling on my leg was unmistakable."

Michael, shaking his shoulders as though he had a cold chill, "that must have been a terrible feeling Mrs. Corning!"

"Yes it was Michael, yes it was."

"Pretty much all night, I found myself waking up kicking my legs up and down and from side to side to get them off of me. When I would catch one of them with a pretty good kick, I could hear it screech and run away. Now I didn't care if they were harmed! I had to get them off me! I began scratching at the limb with my left hand trying to bait them from my leg. When I could feel one of them smelling at my hand, I would hold it very still until I was sure I could catch it. A couple of times they actually bit my hand before I was sure. Anyway, when I was sure, I would grip down just as hard as I could and reach it over to my other hand where I could get it around the throat. Of course it was trying to save its own life, so it would rip its claws into my arms trying to force me to turn it loose. But I continued to squeeze until I was certain it was dead. It would stop thrashing with its claw, and would hang lifeless in my hands. Then, I would toss it off the boulder behind me and start the process all over again when I felt one on my leg."

"I'd find myself dozing off and occasionally one would bite at me before I would realize that they were on me. Certainly not a pleasant way to be awakened, I assure you. I managed to make it through the night and with the daylight I felt much safer."

"Dew formed on the leaves overnight and because my hands were free, I was able tear leaves off and lick the moisture from them. I was hungry, but at least I wasn't hungry and thirsty. I was also able to use the dew to cleanse the wounds on my hand and arms a little. I had a few places on my left hand that were chewed up pretty bad, but it was nothing compared to what those claws had done to my arms. My right arm was, by far, in the worse condition. It looked as though someone had taken a razor knife and just sliced away at me with it. It was pretty painful, but much to my surprise there really wasn't a lot of blood noticeable."

The Convention

"From time to time, I could hear the helicopter flying over the area. Of course, I knew they were looking for me. At the same time though, I knew a helicopter would never spot me. The leaves on the limb were far too thick and pretty much covered my entire body. No, - - I knew that if I were going to be found, it was going to be from a search team on the ground with a sharp, sharp eye."

"The light of the day did give comfort, but it also brought about the flies. Now I was young, but I knew exactly what was going on. The flies were eating from the bitten areas of my leg and laying eggs in the flesh - - that's just what flies do. I was really pretty fortunate though, because I could hear much more flies around the bodies of the animals I had thrown behind me, than were actually getting on me. There was no way I could keep the flies off my leg, so I didn't concern myself with it. They about drove me crazy with my hands and arms though. It was a constant battle swinging my arms and hoping they would just go to the dead animals."

"I'll tell you Michael, the heat was as unbearable during the day as the animals were during the night, just awful! I actually found myself wanting the sun to go down. You've heard the old saying, 'be careful what you ask for'?"

"Sure," Michael said with every ounce of his attention focused on her.

"Well Michael, I got what I asked for, the sun did go down. I was hoping against all odds that the animals would forget I was there, but they didn't, they returned."

"Mrs. Corning, you've got to be kidding me! I remember my father talking to my mother about a similar story when I was a teenager. I didn't hear all the details, but I remember them talking about how the lady was a missionary and wouldn't be able to pay for the doctor bills. I remember they sat down and wrote a short note for the lady and placed it in an envelope along with some money to help out with the doctor bills."

"Oh how precious, I just love stories like that. Maybe it's the same story. I remember the story did make the news. That was my 15 minutes of fame," she said with her polite little wink. "Do you want me to continue Michael, or would you prefer talking about something else?"

"I'll tell you Mrs. Corning, I'd appreciate you finishing the story for me. This is a story I want to share with my brothers."

"Well... okay."

"Soon after the sun went down, the animals returned, - - they returned and they were smarter! I believe that a couple of them had used their rest time to figure out how they were going to claim me. Initially, one tried crawling on my legs and again I would start kicking my legs frantically if I couldn't coax it to my hand. This worked for a while, but soon they began to position themselves in the crevice of the boulder and bite. I could feel them tearing my clothing and eventually the flesh loose from my leg - - and I could hear them chewing - - at times - - even swallowing. I knew that I had killed four of them, and eventually reasoned that there were, whatever they were, at least three of them left. Well there was nothing I could do - - nothing but pray, cry, and wait to die. I did get comfort from praying and it didn't take me too long to figure out that crying wasn't helping. It wasn't stopping them, and it wasn't stopping the pain."

"I had been praying, but that's when I began to pray hard. I stopped my crying and I prayed for my family members, my friends and most of all for the children of the village. Quite frankly, I felt it might have been "my time" and those poor children couldn't take care of themselves. I prayed for things that I wanted forgiveness for and then I asked God to rescue me from this situation."

"After I finished that prayer, a couple of the animals began fighting - - I could hear them making quite a bit of noise. I originally thought they were fighting over best placement, but I soon came to realize they were fighting over getting off of the boulder the fastest. I was confused at their sudden exit. Then, I felt fear in the air."

"I didn't realize he was there, until that horrifying breathing was right beside my head. I had been living in this area for close to a year and had no idea a tiger could move about so quietly. My right arm was lying down on the boulder, with my elbow bent and my hand near my head.

My left arm was positioned across my chest. He sniffed my face a few times - - I was absolutely petrified. I wanted to act as though I was dead, but he had seen my eyes and he knew I was alive. He continued sniffing down my neck and chest, pushing my arm out of his way with his nose and pausing occasionally to look back at my face. He looked over the limb, continuing to sniff, until he found what he was looking for. Apparently, there was more blood on my leg than I had imagined. He took a step forward, preparing to go over the limb. When he did, his rear paw was directly on top of my right arm between the shoulder and the elbow, right about here," as she pointed. "The pressure exerted from his weight was so great that it forced blood up through the scratches on my forearm. He stepped on over the limb and his weight left my arm. That was quite a relief, until he started licking at the wounds."

"Well I knew what was coming, so I made my peace with God and began praying again. While I was praying, I felt the weight of his body as he stretched out along side my leg. I couldn't see him, but it was unmistakable. He stretched out there beside my leg with his head resting in the direction of the stream. I reasoned that he wasn't hungry right now, but knew that he would be eventually. He was just laying claim to me."

"All night long I was far too afraid to sleep Michael. I just lay there listening to him breath. Occasionally, I would see him raise his head up and look around as if he had heard something. He would focus his head in a specific direction with his eyes peering off into the distance, just as still as a statue. Then as suddenly as he would raise his head, he would lay it back down. I remember praying that he would quit hearing things - - that he would continue sleeping. I knew if he was sleeping, I was living."

"Somehow, I did finally sleep. I don't know for how long though. I just remember the morning sun hitting my face through the leaves. When I opened my eyes, I saw him lift his head up and open his mouth with a long yawn. Michael his teeth, you couldn't believe how big. He looked directly at my face. Well, the last thing I wanted to do was intimidate him. I closed my eyes as fast as I could. I could feel the tears falling down my cheeks. That's when I felt his paw on my lower leg as he stood up. The claw was pointed towards my foot though. I opened my eyes to the extent of a squint. He was looking away from me. He walked to the edge of the boulder and jumped down towards the stream. Well, I just couldn't believe it! He was leaving me there. I started thanking God and my emotions just ran away. I don't think I had ever cried that much."

"So there I was, I had survived the night with a wild tiger sleeping right beside me. I was still trapped, hungry, thirsty, the sun was rising with every minute, and flies were returning. I was not about to wish for nightfall again though, no way!"

"Sometime later in the day, I don't know what it was, for some reason I decided to look over to my left. That's when I had the worst of my fears during the daylight. Hyenas! Six of them, about 100 yards off, and they were staring at me. I don't know how they saw me under that branch, but they sure did. A couple of them took a few steps toward me and I heard a growl coming from below. The tiger hadn't left. He was down under the boulder, out of the sun. He was simply guarding me until his appetite returned."

"When the hyenas heard him, they stopped dead in their tracks. The problem was, they didn't retreat. They just sat down and continued looking at me."

"Now, I'm hoping that six hyenas can't scare off a tiger who is saving me for dinner before I die of infection in the wounds from the scavengers, thirst or hunger. It may not make a lot of sense to you, but I was starting to hope for the tiger. I knew they generally went for the throat; at least that would be quick."

"But at the moment, thirst was in the lead. I was so thirsty - - my mouth and throat felt like a cotton ball. Well, they weren't very tasty, but it was all I had, I began pulling leaves from the branch, one at a time, to eat. I hoped that there would be some moisture inside the leaves. Just the chewing of the leaves helped to form some saliva in my mouth which, of course, relieved the dryness. Maybe there wasn't enough moisture to keep me alive, I didn't know. But I also felt like if there wasn't enough moisture, that might not be such a bad thing. At least, not as long as it happened before the tiger returned. I ate leaves from the branch all day long and still did not feel as though I had eaten anything.

And the sun, it was again just so incredibly hot; but against my wishes, I could see, would be setting soon."

"My face continued to be hot for quite a while after the sun went down, so I knew I must have had a sun burn. I remember thinking that I needed to get some cream for my face. I think I was losing it at the time. I glanced over to my left and sure enough, the hyenas were gone. I figured this meant that my tiger must still be below me keeping guard over his claim. Unfortunately, I was right. I heard loud rustling below me and within a matter of moments there he was. He walked up to me within two feet of my face and looked directly into my eyes."

"I don't know, I guess I'd had all I could take. I didn't close my eyes - - I stared as hard as I could right back at him. I wanted to make him mad, I wanted this over! He bent his head down to mine, his nose touching my cheek while he sniffed and made a loud, gruff sound in his throat. Then I could feel his nose on my throat, pushing against my chin several times. Well, I closed my eyes figuring this was it and I prayed my final prayer again. During my prayer, I felt him pull away from me. I continued praying, but couldn't help opening my eyes to see what he was doing. He stepped over the limb and sniffed at my wounds. I felt him begin licking at one of them. About that time, he sunk his fangs deep into my leg. It was a slow, forceful bite as though he had spotted a choice piece of flesh and wanted only that portion to begin his meal. He began shaking his head from side to side ripping at the meat. I could tell the bite was in the most muscular part of my upper leg, and I could see my foot flopping from side to side until he tore the flesh loose. He raised his head up and looked in my eyes, my flesh hanging from one side of his mouth. He then lowered his head and began chewing it. I must have passed out at that point. The sun had only recently gone down and I was being awakened by the sun coming up. I tried reaching my head up to see over the limb, to see if he was there, but I couldn't see over it. Then off in the distance I saw the monkeys in the trees. Many of them were looking towards me and the boulder. That's all I needed to know, he was there, but hadn't woke up."

"Suddenly, I heard voices calling my name. Of course this was bitter sweet, because I could hear them yelling for me and I couldn't yell back to them. Before long they were literally close enough that if I had a stone, I could have probably thrown it in their general direction and gotten their attention."

"I rubbed my hands back and forth frantically on the boulder searching for anything to throw out to make some noise significant enough for them to hear... there was nothing. I could tell that they were passing by me. I never felt so helpless, but this was somewhat of a blessing; while the tiger was sleeping, he wouldn't be a threat to the people searching for me and he was not eating me alive."

"I thought to myself 'Lord help me to get their attention without this tiger waking up'. Just then, I felt the worst of the bites. I could feel the teeth hit against my thigh bone and grind across it while he bit down several times. I'm sure he was trying to take my leg completely off, the pain was just horrible. I reached out and grabbed one of the branches and pulled it down to my mouth. I began biting on the branch and squeezing and shaking it as hard as I could to help myself deal with the pain. I just shook it and shook it until I couldn't feel the pain anymore. That's when I felt the hand of one of the children touching my shoulder. I looked over and could see his head and arms extending above the top of the boulder. His precious little eyes looked into mine and he started crying and hugging me and all the while he was yelling to the others 'I have her, I have her.'

"The child and I then heard the tiger begin to growl in a very low pitch. It was a low, but enormously powerful pitch. I could feel the vibration of it on the boulder. I tried to yell to him, but my mouth and throat was so dry, all I could do was whisper through tears, 'there's a tiger on the other side of the limb. Run! Run!' I could see the fear expressed by his eyes. He jumped down from the boulder right away."

"The tiger stood up, but didn't go after him, he just stood there. I remember that it gave me comfort when the tiger didn't follow him. The tiger laid back down finishing what he was doing. I was completely out of tears, completely out of fear, completely out of pain... I was literally numb. Within just a few minutes, I heard the child returning. This time his father was with him though. The next thing I know, his father is standing on the boulder looking directly at the tiger who was again standing. He had a long stick and had put a sharp point on it with his knife. With the stick in one hand and a knife in the other, he stood up to that tiger. The roar was unbelievable and he was swatting at him with his claws. If his father was frightened, he sure didn't show it. It was the bravest thing I'd ever seen. He lunged at the tiger, screaming to the top of his lungs with the stick pointed directly at its face and forced the point directly onto his nostril."

"That's all it took. The tiger shook his head back and forth, jumped from the boulder in the direction of the stream, and ran off through the brush. I was rescued! The child made his way up again, hugged and kissed me telling me that he had heard the leaves from the branch shaking. By the time the others got there, he and his father had looked at my arms and leg, given me a drink of water and used the remainder to pour over the wounds."

"I knew instantly how bad it was by the expressions on their faces. I would have given anything for that poor child not to have seen that. I almost wished he hadn't found me at all."

"You know, five little children and two adults got that limb off of me. I felt so relieved, but that brought about another problem. I started bleeding pretty bad when the pressure of the limb was removed. They packed the wounds with pieces of their new shirts we had given them. I was numb from the waist down, but with the limb out of the way, I could see the damage done while they were bandaging me, that is, when I had the courage to look. Those precious little children actually ripped up shirts and then tied the clothing around and over the wounds to stop the bleeding. They were really quite impressive the way the handled themselves, and me. In what I felt like was the worst wound, I could see the cavity where a portion of my leg used to be - - muscle hanging over the outside and I could see the bone extending through. It was obvious that the bone had been clawed or chewed somewhat, but it was intact."

"The adults had sent the children to gather long sticks and vine. When they returned, they used the sticks and vine to fashion a stretcher. The adults and the children removed their pants and stretched them out on the stretcher to provide some padding for me to lay on."

The Convention

"As I laid there looking at them, I found that I had many more tears left. I realized that I hadn't given those people anything that they really needed other than my love for them. I was crying because of the love they were showing for me at the time. It wasn't that he hadn't shown fear to the tiger, it was the love he had shown for me. I was crying because of how blessed I was. People who I had known only about a year, loved and cared for me so much that they had given back the clothing, the only possessions they had, to me."

"Well, they used the remainder of the vine as rope tying it to each corner of the stretcher and with the children stationed at varying levels of the tree, they lowered me to the ground."

"Eventually they got me back to the village. My husband was off with another search crew and couldn't be reached in time to see me off. The helicopter pilot also had a medical background from serving in war and convinced everyone that we needed to go right away. He explained that there wouldn't be room on his helicopter anyway. All the villagers were standing around as they prepared to put me in. All of the children had picked me a wild flower and bundled them together at the base. Knowing I would probably never see them again, the tears were flowing like the dew dripping from the trees. And with that, they placed my stretcher on the helicopter and I was on my way to the hospital."

"Well, as you can imagine Michael, the injuries were quite significant. The doctors did what they could for me, but the damage was beyond their abilities - - all they could do was stabilize me. It was necessary for me to get back to the states for the care I needed. They had a medical team accompany me on an airplane to take care of me during the flight. I slept most of the way, but I remember them being so kind to me. I held the flowers against my chest all the way there."

"When we arrived at the hospital, they rushed me in and removed the bandages and my flowers so they could assess the damage and figure out what they were going to do. I don't think the doctors thought I could hear them… but I could. I heard them saying that I was not going to make it because of my weakened state, and how bad the wounds were. The youngest doctor there explained the worst of the wounds to another doctor, saying it was the size of a six inch circle with about three inches of my thigh bone completely exposed. I knew right away this was the same wound I had seen. He explained that there were scratches on the bone, both from teeth and claws, and that it (my leg) was already showing signs of a severe infection. He was convinced my leg would have to be amputated. Then he said that I was an absolute miracle that he would never get a chance to talk with. In other words, it was a miracle I had lasted as long as I did, but he also thought I wasn't going to pull through. I was so frightened."

"Well, they finished prepping me for surgery and off I went. I remember being in the operating room and the doctor placing the mask over my face, looking at me and telling me everything would be fine. I remember not believing his eyes… I don't remember anything else."

"The next thing I knew, I woke up and my father gave me this necklace. It made me feel so incredibly special. The love he expressed to me was just wonderful. I have never taken it off and I can tell you Michael - - since that moment, I have not been frightened of anyone or anything - - not even for a moment."

"Mrs. Corning, that is without a doubt the most horrifying story I have ever heard," Michael stated with virtual disbelief. "But at the same time, it's very beautiful. You are certainly much stronger than me and you obviously proved those doctors wrong. I don't think I could have made it through that! I mean, how can a person possibly live through three days of something so horrific?"

"God, Michael, God! God got me through those nights! God got me through those days! God heard my prayers and God sent that sweet little child to my rescue! There is no question Michael, God!"

"I can tell you Mrs. Corning, you wear the necklace very well. It's really very pretty. I like the way each silver 'A' leans back and attaches to the other two to form the pyramid shape. I can tell the 'A's' are sitting on a gold foundation, but what is that on the inside of the 'A's'? I can see something in there, I just can't quite make it out?"

"Oh, you mean the stone Michael? That's a sapphire - - isn't it beautiful? Look at it closely."

Michael leaned in a little to get a better look.

"Even closer than that Michael, look closely."

"Wow," Michael said with his eyes open, as if he were a child opening a present. "How is that possible… it looks as though it's suspending itself in the center, without touching anything? That's pretty wild!"

"Quite amazing, isn't it?" she said with a perfect smile. "I'm not quite sure how it floats like that. You know you're one of very few I've ever shown that feature to, you should be honored Michael. Have you ever in your life seen a stone that shade of blue?"

"No, I don't believe I have. But I'll tell you Mrs. Corning, I consider myself honored just to be able to sit here and chat with you. Tell me, did your father come up with the design for the necklace?"

"He sure did - - he did it for me. That's why I love it so."

"He must have put an enormous amount of effort into that necklace. Obviously, he loves you very much."

"Oh definitely! I have never been so positive of anything."

"Answer something for me, if you don't mind Mrs. Corning."

"I'll try my very best Michael, what is it?"

"During all that time on the boulder and what you went through - - you prayed and the start of your prayer was for other people, and then you asked forgiveness for your sins, and finally for rescue. Most people would probably ask for help out of the situation they were in first. Why did you pray in the order that you did? I mean, you must be some kind of a saint Mrs. Corning."

"Far from it Michael - - far from it. I knew my fate was in the hands of God and I just loved them so. I wanted to do anything I could to look out for them. I don't think I did anything you wouldn't have done given a similar situation Michael."

"I don't know about that," Michael said turning his head from side to side with a look of utter amazement in his eyes. "I don't know about that. Well, if you don't mind I'll finish checking your leg while we chat?"

"You go right ahead Michael. You go right ahead."

"Does it hurt anywhere that I'm touching your leg?" Michael asked while making eye contact, looking for the first hint of discomfort.

"No, not yet. The pain is actually further up my leg though Michael."

"About where at?"

"Here, just above my knee," she said as she placed her hand over it.

"Is there any chance I'm going to hurt you where the animal bites were?"

"Oh don't you worry about that, my leg healed perfectly many years ago."

"Perfectly! With the wounds you described, I would think you wouldn't even have a leg right now. In fact, I don't mind telling you, I looked to see if your other leg was fake. I don't want to keep you talking about this if it's uncomfortable for you, but how were they able to fix it?"

"God, Michael, God! No one else could have possibly fixed the damage done. I mean, I appreciated the work that the doctors did for me, but it was well above their means. No, it was God who healed my injuries Michael, God."

Michael nodded his head in agreement, placed one hand under her knee and positioned the other immediately over the area that Mrs. Corning had pointed to. While doing so, he could feel some deformity in the leg and was certain that she had, in fact, broken her leg.

"Well Mrs. Corning, I have good news and bad news."

Chuckling a little laugh, "Okay Michael, give me the bad news."

"I believe you're correct about your leg, it's broken."

"And the good news Michael?"

"Well, you take pain very well and this is nothing compared to the things you've overcome."

"Yes! I guess that is good news Michael," she stated agreeably.

"Well, if you don't mind Mrs. Corning, I'm going to try and find something to splint your leg, so I can carry you downstairs?"

"Now Michael, God love ya'! I can tell you're a very strong man and in my younger days I would have probably faked an injury for the chance to have you carry me, you're so handsome. Let's be honest though - - even with those baggy clothes on, I think we can both agree that I outweigh you by a significant amount. Sorry Michael, I just don't think you're quite that strong. Now if a person could carry another on looks, you could carry me a mile."

"Why Mrs. Corning, a petite little thing like you," he said smiling. "You know, I work out pretty often - - I might just surprise you."

"Oh, ha ha - - Michael you are such a kind man, such a kind man. Whew, it's getting a little hot in here," as she fanned her hand in front of her face. "It'd be nice if we had some air circulating in here."

"Yea, I'm with you Mrs. Corning, some air would sure be nice. Well if you don't mind, I think I'll just sit down here beside you for awhile and we can wait together for someone."

"That's very sweet Michael. I really think I'll be fine. If you want, I can just wait here and you can go call for help - though I don't mind telling you Michael, I'd feel a whole lot better if we had more light in here. I tend to prefer light over darkness."

"If what happened to you had happened to me, I'd probably sleep with every light in the house on and you could forget about camping trips - - no way! You know Mrs. Corning, I think you and I are a lot alike with regard to our fathers. I sure love him. Not just because he was always there for me when I was growing up, and heck - - even now, but also because of the way he is regarded by friends of the family and the community as a whole. Yea Mrs. Corning, my father is the man I aspire to be."

"What do you mean Michael?"

Jeff T. Travis

CHAPTER FOUR – THE HITCHHIKER

"Well, I have thought about this from time to time," he said, pausing from what he was doing. "As much as I've thought about it, I've never been able to recall a single time where my father ever hesitated to help another person, no matter the circumstances. My father is the type who will stop at nothing to help someone in need. Once I remember, we were on our way to visit some family friends in Missouri. I was 14 years old and we were in Ohio heading west on I-70. This was during Thanksgiving and it was pretty cold outside. My father mentioned to my mother, that there was a matured man standing alongside the interstate hitchhiking. My father said, 'it sure is cold outside to being doing that.' My mother just smiled because she knew what was coming next. She looked back and said, 'Move your stuff, because we're getting ready to have company.' My father took the very next exit and headed back towards the man."

"Headed back? My goodness, you mean the man was headed the other way?"

"Yea, he sure was. My father pulled over and the man walked up to us at a fast pace. My mother rolled down her window and my father stretched across her so he could make first contact with the man."

"It's pretty cold outside Mr. – where ya headed?"

"I'll sure agree its cold out here. I'm on my way to Pittsburg."

"Pittsburg you say, that's exactly where we're headed," as he turned his head in my direction giving a quick wink. "If you like, you'd sure be welcome to come along. We can chat and keep each other company to help pass the time."

"The man's face lit up with approval and he said, 'yes sir, I'll take you up on that... but only if you'll let me pay for part of the gas, I know how expensive it is'."

"My father nodded his head in agreement and with that, the man got in on my side and we were on our way."

"As soon as we pulled back onto the interstate, my father introduced all of us looking at the man through the rear view mirror and told him to make himself comfortable."

The man situated his belongings taking care not to put things where they would be in the way.

"Nice to meet you fine people," he said with a smile. "Name's Willie Hanover. I sure thank you good folks for picking me up. I'm beginning to realize that I'm not quite as tough as I used to be. The cold never used to bother me, but anymore, I'm finding the warmer it is, the more I like it. The snow sure is pretty out there though. I'm on my way to see my daughter. I just lost my wife, well my second wife, to cancer two months ago. I think my daughter is really just now coming to terms with it and she needs me there to help her through it."

"We spent our life savings trying to pull her through the cancer, but it just wasn't to be. Barbara kept telling me that if I kept on I'd be destitute and she just wanted to go without having to worry about me. At a time like that, she was thinking about me and how I would be after she was gone. I've been so fortunate in my life," Willie said as his eyes began to tear up. "I actually had two women in my life that I loved, and who loved me. I lost my first wife many years ago to a terrible tragedy. We were only married two years, but those two years were wonderful. I didn't think I could ever love again after her. But then I met Barbara. I really loved her," he said while beginning to cry.

I put my hand on his shoulder to get his attention and asked him if he wanted a piece of my candy bar. When he looked at me, his tears were quickly replaced with his smile and he continued telling us about his life.

"I had a good job of nineteen years - - excellent pay and benefits. When I was unable to report to work while caring for my wife, they said they had to let me go. The company had put me on paid leave for a little while, but that time ran out. The company explained to me that there was no more paid time for me and that I needed to return to work now. This was the woman that I loved though. I just couldn't bear the thought of someone other than me caring for my Barbara. Someone else had to care for my first wife because I wasn't there. I vowed that would never happen again. No sir! If I was fortunate enough to find another woman who would have me, no one was going to take care of her but me." He began to tear up again while his thumb was pointed in towards his chest, but quickly dried his eyes and regained his composure.

"'I just can't accept welfare, that's what my company said I should 'explore'. There are people in far worse shape than me and most of them are making it, and the ones who aren't making it can use it far more than me. Nope, I've made up my mind. If it comes down to it, I'll live on the streets and work odd jobs to get by."

"Why don't you just get another job?"

The Convention

"Well young man, it's not the easiest thing to explain. I really can't get any meaningful full time employment because of my age, I'm pushing sixty. You know, I don't quite understand the thinking behind that though - - never have. If someone would hire me, they would see that I am strong enough and in good enough shape that they'd get a good five to ten years out of me. They would certainly not have to worry about me being late or not showing up, heck, I was raised better than that. My dad would skin me alive if someone gave me an opportunity and I didn't do right by them. I did right by that company for nineteen years, just as I did right by my Barbara. Don't get me wrong, I appreciate what they did for me, but I gave them my all for nineteen years. When I really needed them, they wouldn't even give me nineteen weeks. I don't know, I just feel like there's a whole lot wrong with that. As an employee, you're expected to be dedicated to the company - - but at the same time - - the company isn't dedicated to the employee. It just didn't used to be that way. Funny how it works out. I'm too old to get a job, but too young and healthy to get my social security. And while I'm too young and healthy for social security, I'm too old to get medical insurance that I can afford. I can't afford it because I don't have a job, and I don't have a job because

Jeff T. Travis

I had to take off work to care for my wife during a time when we needed the insurance. But you know what, it's going to be fine. After I help my daughter through this, I'll get back on my feet. Yes sir, one thing I have surely learned is that life is about doing what's right."

"Over the next four and a half hours we listened and spoke with Willie" Michael explained to Mrs. Corning. "To this day, I'm really not sure who helped who the most during that drive to Pittsburg. I am certain of a couple of things though Mrs. Corning - - I will never forget his smile and optimistic attitude. I mean, obviously he was having difficulty with the passing of his wife, but at the same time, given all the other conversations we shared, it was easy to see that this man was strong in his faith and that he would be fine."

"When we got to Pittsburg, my father insisted on dropping him off at his daughters' house. Of course he stuffed the money Willie had given him for gas, along with a little note, into the front pouch of his bag. I saw him hurrying to write the note as Willie was trying to gather his things. I don't know what the note said, but knowing my father it would have been something to give Willie hope. None of us ever heard from Willie again, but I like to think that he continues to live there to this day."

"So you see Mrs. Corning, if my father can drive an additional nine hours to help someone, and I aspire to be like him, there is no way I could even consider leaving you alone. Besides," Michael said chuckling, "if my brothers got wind that I had left you alone, they would whoop me like there was no tomorrow. So, I think we could protect each other. If you would agree to my sitting here with you until someone else comes by, I can comfort you in this darkness and you can save me from a whoopin'. In all fairness though, you have pretty much proved to me that you can get through anything, so I guess when it all boils down, it should probably be called a well planned and selfish self preservation initiative on my part."

Mrs. Corning laughed for a moment and just as suddenly as she laughed, she became very serious. Michael could see in her eyes that she was about to say something to him that she regarded as important.

"I can tell you come from a very good family Michael. You know, I would say it's a pretty safe bet that you are more like your father than you think you are."

"Well, I appreciate you saying that Mrs. Corning, but if you knew me and my father better, I think you'd agree that I am lacking in many areas. I'm trying, but lacking. Believe me Mrs. Corning, while my father was firm while I was growing up, he was also the single most loving person you'd ever meet. To this day, no matter what the circumstances, if someone needs help, he is always there. Even after we had dropped Willie off and driven back into Ohio, about five miles west of where we had picked Willie up, there was a terrible crash that had involved several cars and a semi truck. You could tell that it had happened much earlier. After all the time we were behind in our travel plans, my father stopped and asked the State Trooper if he needed any help. Of course the trooper said no, that he was only waiting there for four more tow trucks and his job would be done. The trooper said it had been a very bad crash and had made for a long day. He thanked my father for stopping and we went on our way."

"He is beginning to show his age and I'll tell you I was very concerned for him until hearing your comments on aging. He still passes on a lot of wisdom to me and others."

"In what way Michael?"

"Well... he retired a couple of years ago, but he still does volunteer work. He does a lot of public speaking for various charities and conventions. He calls me on the phone all the time, giving me advice on things related to my job - he retired from the same line of work I'm in and..."

"So you took on the same work as your father, how special. I'll bet he's very proud of you Michael."

"Yea, anytime he hears about something I did, he gives me a call on the phone to tell me how proud he is of me. I wouldn't trade my job for the world. My father always told me if I found a job I liked, I wouldn't work a day in my life - - I'd enjoy it too much to call it work. Anyway, my point is that after your comment, he's not sharing and doing all of this just to share and do it, he's sharing and doing it because he cares and as long as he cares, he's not getting older, he's getting wiser and even more in tune with the really important things."

"Now you're catching on Michael, now you're catching on."

"It really puts things in perspective and takes away a lot of the worry I have for him. Heck, for that matter now that I think about it, I probably worry more about my wife and children than I need to. I'm sure that I will share the same analogy with my children some day."

"I found these in my pack Mrs. Corning, let me see if they will work as a splint for your leg real quick, so we can be ready when someone comes by. I'm going to be as gentle as I can Mrs. Corning, but I'm afraid it may hurt for a minute."

"You go right ahead Michael, I can handle it. You mentioned your wife and children. What is your wife's name and how many children do you have Michael?"

The Convention

"My wife's name is Lynn and I have three beautiful boys - - Thomas, Anthony, and Cole. They're thirteen, ten and six."

"I'm sure they're just wonderful Michael. You can always tell about another persons' family by the way the face and eyes light up when they tell another person about them. I could see it in your face and eyes even in this darkened area - - I can tell you love them very much. I'll tell you Michael, as long as you follow the rules and you instill the three keys in your children, you truly have nothing to worry about. Neither you, nor your wife and children will ever be presented with more than you can handle."

"What are rules and the three keys Mrs. Corning?"

"The good Lords' Commandments and faith, hope and love Michael. Faith, hope and love."

Michael smiled. That comment made him feel good. He knew that he had always pressed for those qualities in his home and the Commandments took priority on the wall in the dining room. At the same time however, he questioned to himself whether or not he was being a good husband and father.

"Michael?"

"Yes. Mrs. Corning."

"What have you done in your life that you would ask God to forgive you for?"

"Well why on earth would you ask me that?"

"I just think back to my experience that night on the boulder that I asked for forgiveness. I felt so relieved at that moment. I sense that you're looking for something, but you don't know what it is, or where to find it. What would you ask forgiveness for?"

"Well if you really want to know Mrs. Corning, I guess the most important thing would be asking forgiveness for not being the husband and father that I should be. I try, believe me I do. I just don't know what I need to be doing to make it right - - to make me feel right. There are several other things too, but I don't think I would feel comfortable talking about it."

"Would you do me a favor Michael?"

"I'll sure do my very best."

"Leave my leg alone for a moment and look at me, look into my eyes. Michael you have helped me so much here today," she said with her hand gently touching his cheek. "I want you to have what I was able to get."

"What's that Mrs. Corning?"

"A tremendous burden lifted from your chest and the removal of torment eating away at your very body and soul. Forgiveness Michael, I want you to have forgiveness!"

"You are amazing Mrs. Corning. First, putting yourself last with the wild animals and now putting yourself last with your broken leg and me. You're quite a woman Mrs. Corning," he said with sincerity. "What do you want me to do?"

"Close your eyes. Go on, close your eyes. Now, I just want you to think about things that you would ask forgiveness for and when you're finished, let me know."

Michael sat there with his eyes closed and his head slightly bowed, submitting to her request. He thought of everything he could think of that he wanted to be forgiven for. Just as she requested, when he was finished he said, "okay, I'm finished."

"Okay. Now Michael, I want you to ask God to forgive you for them and when you finish asking him, finish by asking it in the name of Jesus Christ. Now you go right ahead, I'll be right here when you're finished. Be sincere Michael, be sincere."

Michael closed his eyes and prayed. After he finished, he opened his eyes and smiled.

Mrs. Corning looked into his eyes and could see the beginnings of tears. She again touched his cheek and said, "Amen!"

"What a beautiful smile you have Michael. Keep wearing that and we won't even need that little flickering light. I'll tell you Michael, people don't know the burden they carry until they allow the good Lord to lift it from their shoulders. If you love the Lord Michael, faith, hope and love will carry you always - - and in all ways."

Mrs. Corning began to fan herself. "What I wouldn't give to have some fresh air blowing through here. Take my hand Michael."

Michael reached to grasp her hand as she had requested. Though he didn't say so, he began to get concerned for her, wondering if perhaps she wasn't going into shock. Suddenly a burst of air made its way through where they were sitting.

"Michael do you feel that - - oh, doesn't that feel wonderful. I'm sharing in your forgiveness."

"My forgiveness? That's air Mrs. Corning. It does feel wonderful tho…

CHAPTER FIVE – THE EMBRACE

Michael shook his head realizing something was wrong. "Mrs. Corning. Mrs. Corning," his voice getting louder and louder each time he yelled for her. "Mrs. Corning, are you there? Something isn't right," he whispered. "It's still dark and I don't think I have moved," as he was feeling around on the floor just in case Mrs. Corning had passed out or something and he just couldn't see her because she was out of his range of vision. But that was not the case, Mrs. Corning was simply not there.

Michael thought to himself, "Wait a minute, where's the handrail and the steps? It's still dark, so I know I'm in the same general location, just a different area. Okay," he said to himself in a reasoning manner, "she had a broken leg - - she couldn't possibly have moved herself and me.

The Convention

Did someone else move us? If we were moved, why did they leave me here? Why don't I remember? At least now I can make out the floor as being slightly grey. Is this because the floor is a different color in this area, or have I finally been here long enough that my eyes have adjusted? Mrs. Corning and I were together for about twenty minutes - - I guess that would be enough time for my eyes to adjust. At least I'm not uncomfortable from the heat anymore." As instantly as that last thought went through his mind, Michael now knew exactly what had happened – he had suffered another blackout.

Being a strong man, Michael had told no one, except for a couple of his brothers that he worked with, of a problem he had been having for about a year where he would periodically blackout. He didn't want anybody to think he wasn't strong, especially his wife and kids, or his boss, because he didn't want to risk losing his job. He had remembered Willie losing his job when he was unable to report for work. More than this, he didn't want his wife to know, because she always worried about him anyway and he did not want to add worry into the life of the woman he loved so very much and was doing more than her part in raising their children. It was for the children as well. Michael knew that the kids could always tell when something was bothering their mother. This always had the same affect on the children, sadness. And this in turn, though she would try to hide it, always had the same affect on Lynn, concealing her feelings and putting on the happy face. The kids could generally see through her though. For these reasons, Michael and his brothers kept the illness to themselves, secretly trying to determine what the problem was. So far, between Michael and his brothers, they had concluded from literature they had read, that he was more than likely suffering from a mild form of epilepsy, sugar diabetes, a brain tumor, or a stress related disorder connected to his job. His brothers had tried to get him to go to the doctor. Michael strictly refused, saying that his wife took care of the bills and she would certainly question him when the bills came in the mail. He agreed that he could credit one or two visits as a physical, beyond the scope of a required work related physical, but explained to his brothers that he felt like it would take several visits to several different doctors and he wouldn't be able to explain several visits away. His wife would hound him, until he broke and the end result would be his entire family worrying. He just didn't want that.

The brothers agreed and had been working with Michael on his diet over the past couple of months, and had each done their part to reduce the amount of stress on Michael. During the entire process, the brothers were also documenting a great deal of information about the blackouts. Strangely, an overwhelming majority of the blackouts had happened in the middle of the day at work. Because of this, Michael and his brothers were becoming more and more convinced that the problem was related to diet or stress. One good thing that came out of it was, because of the general time frame of the blackouts, his brothers were able to cover for him. Most of the time the blackouts would only last about a minute, other times, they would last much longer.

Michael did recall one time when he was at the mall doing some Christmas shopping when he suffered a blackout. Afterwards, Michael found himself three blocks away in the park. He had no idea how he had gotten there, or how long he had been there. He did get a clue from his wife when he returned home and she stated "my goodness honey, I can't remember you ever putting this much time into Christmas shopping - - you've been gone for over two hours". Although this was very concerning to Michael, he said nothing, smiled and walked into the other room. He knew he had gone to the mall only to pick up a t-shirt that his son Anthony had seen a week before and really liked. He then reasoned that he could have been 'out' for as much as an hour and didn't even have the shirt he went after. He may have bought it, but didn't have it then, he just didn't know.

Because of this, Michael then became even more concerned for Mrs. Corning. He wondered if perhaps he had simply left her. Was she okay? Was she still lying back there in pain and frightened of the dark? Was she questioning me as to why I was leaving her and all the while I was walking away from her as if I were ignoring her, but her not realizing I couldn't hear her? Did I help her downstairs before I blacked out? Why did this blackout have to happen now? I wish I would have acted on her idea and left to get help. I'm so stupid! At least then I might have reached someone before I blacked out. I've let her down. Michael made up his mind then and there that he was going to find Mrs. Corning. He stood up and began to walk. Still dark, Michael could

The Convention

not see much of anything except for the slightly grey floor amidst the dark black walls off in the distance. He walked for only a few moments when he heard it, a voice calling his name.

"Michael." _____ "Michael."

The voice was coming from his left. A very soft and gentle voice.

"Michael, _____ Michael, _____ come this way Michael."

Michael shouted, "I'm coming Mrs. Corning, I'm coming. I was afraid that I wouldn't find you," Michael said while he went in the direction the voice was coming from. The voice could be heard easier and easier with each step he took and likewise, he could begin to put a shape together. He could see this woman was standing and realized immediately, this was not Mrs. Corning.

"Hello Michael," he heard.

"Oh hello," Michael replied about five feet away from her. "I was hoping to see a woman that I knew. I can tell by your voice and features that you are much younger than the lady I am looking for. Have you by chance seen or heard of an older lady, about sixty around here named Mrs. Corning? I think she needs help and I, I, well I was with her, but can't seem to find her now."

"No Michael, I'm sorry I haven't."

Michael was wondering to himself if perhaps he had met this woman during his blackout and didn't remember her. "I can't see your face very clearly - - you kept calling my name... have we met?" Michael asked, not wanting her to think he didn't remember her if they had just met.

"One thing I've learned around here is that anything is possible!" the woman said excitedly.

"How do you know my name?"

"Your father is going to be speaking soon and he wanted me to come out here and wait on you to escort you in. It's my lucky day. I called for you just a couple of times and there you were, almost close enough to touch."

Pausing with his fingers on his left hand touching his forehead, Michael reasoned to himself that his father often spoke at various public engagements. While his father had not told him of any upcoming speaking events, he didn't want to seem as if he wasn't aware that his father was speaking. Until he could make sense of things, he figured the best thing to do would be to go with her and hopefully figure it out there. Besides, if his father was looking for him, he was obviously where he was supposed to be.

The woman, now within a single step of Michael said, "My name is Lillian, I'm so very pleased to meet you Michael." She placed one hand over Michael's right shoulder and the other hand around his waist, embracing him as though she had known him forever.

Michael thought to himself how beautiful Lillian was with her long blonde hair hanging over her shoulders and falling down to near her waist. Somewhere in her mid twenties, she had the bluest eyes he had ever seen. Her smile was the kind of smile that makes it easy for people to approach her - - glistening, yet humble. The actual embrace was so incredibly warm and tender. Michael immediately likened the feeling to some of the most touching moments of his life and he began reflecting on them. The thoughts were racing rapidly through his mind, but he could make perfect sense of every thought and was visualizing the thoughts as fast as he was thinking them.

It was his ninth birthday. The kitchen was decorated with the touch only achieved by his loving mother. The colors chosen were the traditional 'birthday boy' blues and reds, but all put together just so perfectly. Balloons and streamers hanging from the ceiling everywhere you looked and on the back of one chair, three balloons. This of course, the seat of honor, was where Michael would sit to open his presents and blow out the candles on his birthday cake. The cake took the shape of his favorite super hero. She loved to bake, so she had plenty of practice. He could actually smell the cake baking while he thought about it. She always let him lick the bowl and always made sure the spoon was heaping with icing.

The Convention

Michael remembered all of his friends being present for all his birthdays, just as he was always present for theirs. His father always insisted on this type of togetherness, "when one celebrates, we all celebrate," he would say. After everyone finished singing happy birthday to him, he began opening presents. Just as any child, this was certainly his favorite part. His friends had each given him a present and he liked all of them. It didn't matter if the gift was purchased from a store or was handmade from paper in their living room the night before.

After he had finished opening the gifts, his mother and father left the room and when they returned, they were holding the most beautiful dog he had ever seen. His father knelt down to the ground holding the pup under the belly and gently sat him on the floor. He remembered feeling overwhelmed and throwing himself to the floor as the pup was running towards him, slipping and sliding all the way due to the tile on the floor. When they finally made contact, it was the single greatest feeling he'd ever had. Instantly, he loved the dog and the dog loved him. He was simply the most beautiful dog in the world.

One day, a few years later while playing with Max in the park, Michael threw a ball for Max to fetch. The ball went further than Michael had wanted it to, hit a tree trunk and went rocketing to the left. Max was well on his way before the ball even hit the tree. Suddenly, Michael could hear the screeching of brakes and the sliding of tires. Michael ran as fast as he could towards the point where Max ran into the street. All the while he was screaming for Max to stay. "Stay Max! Max - - Stay!" When Michael got to the other side of the trees he could see a man kneeling in front of a car and could hear him saying, "I'm sorry young man, I didn't see him."

Michael could see right away that Max had been hit by the car. He ran to him as fast as he could. He knelt down and hugged him, "it'll be okay boy, it'll be okay". Max was alive, but it was obvious he was hurt very bad. Without hesitation, Michael picked him up and began walking, knowing that the hospital was only four blocks away. He recalled Max not making it to the hospital, dying in his arms about a block from the hospital. Michael stopped and placed Max down gently on the grass stroking his head. The police had been called and while on their way

The Convention

to the accident site, he observed young Michael stretched out beside Max obviously crying. The policeman pulled his cruiser over against the curb next to Michael and Max, got out of the car and approached him. It was obvious to the officer that the dog was dead.

"Hello young man."

"Hello sir."

"Nice dog you got there."

Michael looked at him in disbelief of the comment and advised the policeman that his dog was dead.

"Dead huh?"

"Yes sir, he just got hit by a car. I was carrying him to the hospital, but I didn't get him there in time."

"Good looking dog - - he has a real strong build. I'll bet he was very high spirited."

"What do you mean?"

"You know, happy all the time, acted like every time you came home from school you had been gone for a month, always wanting to run and play... that kind of stuff."

"You're sure right about that. You're right about all of it. How do you know that?"

"Hmmm? That high spirited and you think he's dead?"

"I don't understand officer, what are you trying to say? Max is dead, I'm sure of it. He hasn't taken a breath in a long time. I closed his eyelids myself."

"Son, I want to tell you something - - something that I have believed ever since I was about your age and my dog died. He was a real high spirited dog too. You know what old Mr. Givens taught me?"

"No, what?"

The Convention

"Old Mr. Givens taught me that a high spirited dog like that doesn't die; his high spirit won't let him. Sure, he may have left this place, but I'm telling you his spirit goes directly into another pup and I guarantee you, your dog will be making some kid very happy within the next day or two. What you need to do is think about the happy times you had with your dog and realize just how happy that high spirited soul is going to make another child. Do you remember when you first got him?"

"Yes sir. Best day of my life."

"Well that's exactly how another child is getting ready to feel. Won't that be wonderful?"

"Yes sir it sure would."

"No son, not would, will! And please, if we meet again, you can call me Bill."

"Okay."

"Now why don't you head on out and let me take care of the dog from here. I promise you son, I'll be very careful with him."

Michael hesitated, but then agreed and after giving the officer a hug, he went home to share the news with his family. While telling his mother, she held him close and reminded him of the five good years with Max. Michael then remembered that because his father had cared enough, he was always able to visit with Max in their backyard where his father, later the following day, had built Max a coffin, buried him, and placed a gravestone. Michael didn't know it until almost ten years later, but his father had taken off work that day so he could make sure he would be able to get the body before anything was done with it. He loved his father so much for doing that.

As rapidly as those thoughts went through his mind, he reflected on his wedding day. He recalled his wife walking down the aisle and how beautiful she was in her dress with the train trailing behind and how lucky he was that she had said 'yes'. It was as though she was standing right in front of him at that very moment. He recalled the kiss after

The Convention

sharing their vows. His thought moved directly into the birth of his first child. He remembered how afraid - - terrified he was before the baby was actually born. He remembered going to birthing classes with Lynn and how happy she was while she was pregnant, showing her belly off at every opportunity. He then remember being in the birthing room holding her hand to steady his nerves.

When little Thomas was born and the doctor handed him to Michael, the fear he had of having the baby was immediately replaced with the fear of what he would do without him. There was no explaining it, it was just that way, plain and simple, he immediately loved this child. He remembered leaning over to kiss Lynn and how warm and relaxed she was. It was truly amazing, but nothing even close to how she lit up inside and out when he handed little Thomas to her. Truly a beautiful sight!

He recalled a couple years later, Lynn telling him they were again expecting a baby just before leaving for vacation. Now he was consumed with fears that he was having a child that he knew he couldn't love as much as little Thomas. While on vacation, he recalled being in

McDonalds in Flagstaff while Lynn waited in the car. Little Thomas standing at 2 years of age and facing him with his little hands reached up and forced down into his front pockets. Just then, little Thomas wanted daddy to swing him, apparently, so he lifted his little legs from off the floor. As he did, and because his hands were in his pockets, his shorts suddenly went straight down to the floor along with little Thomas' hands tangled up in the pockets. He recalled bending over trying to get his hands free so he could pull his shorts up and how much little Thomas, along with a restaurant full of people were laughing. The laughing continued even after they ordered and received their food and were walking out to the car with other customers walking behind them laughing, which kept little Thomas laughing right along with them. When they got back in the car, Lynn asked what everybody was laughing about while they were leaving. Little Thomas quickly informed Lynn, "I pulled down my Daddy's pants". Michael then told Lynn the whole story and he remembered how much she laughed while she put her hand on his shoulder telling him it was okay. The only time he could remember her laughing more than that was when he was lying on the floor on his back one day holding little Thomas up in the air playing with him. He remembered Lynn saying "you shouldn't do that right after he eats." He recalled ignoring her and continued laughing and smiling with the baby. He remembered that he wished his mouth would have been shut at that moment. Lynn laughed hysterically while he was gagging. Little Thomas had thrown up directly in his mouth with the accuracy of a professional sniper.

Soon little Anthony was to be born. As with Thomas, Michael recalled being in the birthing room. This time his fear was that he could not possibly love another child as much as his little Thomas. He had expressed this concern to Lynn and she had tried to assure him that it would be okay. He remembered that when little Anthony came into this world and was handed to him by the doctor, he was relieved to feel the immediate love for this baby. He recalled being very happy, it truly was the same love he felt for Thomas. Handing Lynn little Anthony and giving her a kiss, it was very obvious that her love could not have been stronger. When little Anthony was about nine months old, he recalled himself lying on the floor playing with him. Again gagging, he recalled Lynn telling him what a slow learner he was while she was wiping away her tears of laughter. He recalled working the night shift when little Anthony was a baby and how he enjoyed taking a short nap on the couch in his favorite sweat pants a little while before work. Little, but plump Anthony, now pulling himself up on things, had grabbed him in the worst possible place and successfully pulled himself on top of his daddy.

A few years later, Lynn again informed him that they would be having a baby. As with Thomas and Anthony, he remembered being in the birthing room holding her hand to steady his nerves. This time however, he knew he would have the same love for this child.

He recalled how much nicer the overall birthing process was that time because of it. When little Cole was born and the doctor handed him to him, there was no surprise - - he immediately loved this child as well. Again, kissing Lynn and handing her the baby, her smile and eyes said more than any words could ever speak. He recalled that he did learn his lesson of playing with the babies so soon after eating. Where and how he slept, he recalled required a couple refresher lessons.

The Convention

He recalled all the good times they had as a family, including the kickball game in the cul-de-sac a week earlier when his youngest son Cole, finally got the courage to play with them for the first time and how his older sons Thomas and Anthony helped to make sure little Cole made it around the bases and cheered him to home base.

A smile gleamed from Michael as he recalled friends moving in down the street and inviting them to church. He recalled he and his wife had talked about finding a church for three or four years, but something had always come up, providing the perfect excuse for not going. Finally, Lynn put her foot down convincing him that the kids needed it. He recalled not being able to argue her point away and the family joining the friends at church, and the visiting resulting in membership. He recalled the sermons provided by Dr. Mark and how each week the sermon seemed to be spoken directly to him, and how very proud he was to stand up front with his three boys that day to be saved and receive baptism with them.

Finally, he recalled sitting there with Mrs. Corning asking God to forgive him for the sins he had committed.

While he didn't say it at the time, he was really very thankful to her for asking him to do that. How she had asked him to do it for her, but how he knew she was really wanting him to do it for himself.

At that moment, Lillian released Michael and took a step back. "Please follow me Michael, I'll take you to where your father is going to be speaking."

"But how can you see to walk in here?"

"It's okay Michael, I know exactly where I'm going. It's been this way for as long as I've been here. Around here, we call it the mood setter. Please give me your hand, it will make it easier for you to follow me."

Michael nodded his head and grasped her hand. When Lillian turned to begin walking, Michael noticed her mannerisms, the way her arm was slightly extended out and the way her hair trailed behind the movement of her body while she was turning. It instantly reminded him of his mother while he was in grade school. First he recalled his mother holding his hand while walking with him to catch the bus each morning. Strange how holding his mothers hand always seemed to take away the fears he had. He recalled coming home from school each day, and there mom would be, waiting with a smile on her face and waving her hand.

"How was your day sweetie?"

"It was good mom."

"Come here and give your mom a great big kiss and let's go to the kitchen and have a little snack."

He remembered how he looked forward to that every day. It made him feel so special. Everyday, he'd give her a kiss and right afterwards she would turn to the counter, hair trailing behind her. Without fail, she would turn back around with one of his favorite snacks.

Mother always tried to do something special every single day. She knew then that loving memories would result from what she was doing, because her mother had done the same for her and she cherished those memories.

That led Michael to begin thinking about his children, again wondering and hoping he was doing half as good a job as his mother and father had done. He knew that Lynn was a true blessing and the real strength of their home as his job kept him away from home. He was certain of that. Certain that she was always beside the children when they were sick, always providing a loving hug when they were sad, always a tender kiss and bandage for a boo boo, and always making a happy day happier with her pleasant smile and offering of a favorite snack.

Just as he was certain that Lynn was a wonderful mother, he was unsure if he was truly a good father. Had he been doing all he could do to make sure that his children had loving and pleasant memories? His job did keep him away from the house a lot, but if this was a problem, he knew he couldn't use it because his father retired from the same line of work he was in. He recalled his father, not only always made time for him, he made the time something special. He remembered his father somehow always made it to sporting events and cheered louder than any other person there. When we won, we all celebrated together. When we lost, we went for ice cream or something that would put a smile back.

After a loss, he would always say the same thing, "If you never lose, you can't truly appreciate winning – losing makes us stronger and helps make winning feel like winning."

Where did he get the strength to work as hard as he did and yet always find time to do all of the important things with his family? He wondered if he would ever be as strong as his father. Retired and still active in the community, still active in volunteer work, still active with me, still a loving husband to his wife making sure that Friday nights are for them, still active with the church, and still speaking at engagements at the request of any organization in existence for the right reasons. While Michael did not know which organization his father was speaking for today, he was certain of two things. His father would take no compensation, and the organization he was speaking for was worth being a part of.

Michael reasoned this is probably why he went into the same line of work as his father. If his father did it for thirty years, it must be noble.

As they were walking, Michael could see a very narrow and vertical light. It resembled a fluorescent bulb standing on its end, only brighter. With each step the light got wider and brighter. Michael could tell that it was a doorway and that it appeared thin because of the angle they were approaching. It also gave him a clearer sense as to just how dark the area was that he was in.

CHAPTER SIX – THE PILLARS

After another five or six steps, Lillian slowed to a stop and released his hand. While standing in the doorway, she turned her body to the side and extended her left arm up in an inviting manner. "We are here Michael, please come in and make yourself comfortable."

"Thank you Lillian for your help, I really appreciate it."

"No need to thank me Michael. I have others to attend to though, so I have to go now."

Before walking through the door, Michael heard voices, several voices coming from his right side off in the distance. He could tell they were male voices, but he couldn't make out what was being said - - it sounded like a foreign language to him. At the same time, the tone of their voices led him to believe that they needed help. Trying to focus his eyes in on where he believed they were, he could notice figures moving around. It looked like maybe two dozen people, but it was too dark to know for sure how many people there were.

"Who are they?" he asked. "It sounds like they may need some help. Give me just a minute Lillian, I'm going to go check on them real quick," he said while turning his body and taking a step.

"Stop Michael! Don't be concerned about them," as she motioned for him to enter. "They are already being addressed."

"Okay," he said while stepping through the doorway. "I just thought I'd give them a hand if they needed it. Well, it was very nice meeting you Lillian. You have some very special qualities about you, and well … I just wanted you to know that."

"Well thank you Michael, that's very kind of you to say. While you don't seem to know it, you have some very special qualities about you as well," as she continued to walk.

"While I don't seem to know it? What do you mean Lillian? Lillian? Just a moment Lillian!"

She had already passed between several people. Michael went directly past the same people Lillian had, but when he looked for her she was nowhere to be found. There were simply so many people there though. She could be standing behind a person within five feet of him and he would probably never know it.

"My goodness," he thought. "There are a lot of people here - - my dad must be speaking to a very hot topic. I need to start looking for clues as to what my dad is going to be speaking about and figure this out before I run into somebody I know. How embarrassing it would be to run in to somebody that I know and they want to talk about it before he starts, and I have no clue as to the topic," he thought.

Giving a quick glance around the room, looking for anything that could give him information, Michael observed that the attendees for the convention were very diverse in gender, age and race. Beyond this, he noticed that it was clearly informal dress. Many of the attendees were dressed in casual attire, though he did notice some who were dressed in work uniforms and still many others who were dressed in suits. All the convention employees were dressed in the same type and general style of clothing as Lillian. The women wore long, loose fitting and pleated lavender like dresses draped down to the floor with shoulder straps. The men employees wore shirts made of the same material as the dresses, were long sleeved and loose fitting as well, but they were a shade of blue. Seeing a male and female employee standing side by side, it was perfect how well each uniform complimented the other. While there was a great deal of employees working, Michael thought to himself that that would certainly make it easier to find Lillian while he was trying to figure this out, because he couldn't see any attendees being dressed in that manner. It was very classy, but at the same time it was perfect for the environment.

The Convention

Everyone there, while somewhat in their own group, was heavily involved in pleasant conversation, smiling and laughing. Michael reasoned that because of this, the topic his father would speak to was probably not related to AIDS, starving children or something else along that line, because people would not be in such a happy go lucky mood before he spoke if it was such a sad or troubling thing. He remembered that as a young adult, his father spoke to a very large group of people about building a strong family life. The mood of the people today was much the same as then.

The room was very large and his eyes were playing tricks on him as he tried to get used to the lighting. The music playing was very tranquil and at the perfect volume. Loud enough that it was easily heard, but soft enough that it was not necessary to speak up over it.

Looking up towards the ceiling, he couldn't quite tell where the lights were coming from, because there were so many stars painted against the black background. At first glance and squinting, all he could tell was that it was a very high ceiling. The ceiling had to bend around the room from one side to the other because there were no support beams anywhere in the room, and the width and length was far too large for horizontal support alone. He just couldn't see well enough to determine the contour. "Brilliant engineering," he thought. "With these high ceilings, amazing, absolutely amazing."

Michael pulled his eyes away to continue searching for clues. The flooring was a very rich shade of blue and reminded him of the necklace Mrs. Corning was wearing. It was a shade of blue that he had only seen one time before, the stone in her necklace. While looking at the floor, he realized there were no chairs. "Man. Talk about standing room only," he thought. "What if someone gets tired of standing?" Though he could tell his feet and legs were quite comfortable. The flooring seemed to absorb pressure very well.

As he followed the floor, from where he was to a point off in the distance, he noticed a couple of his brothers standing together. They were on the other side of the room standing near a large gathering of people. He started walking in their direction, weaving in and out of people and short pillars. The pillars, hundreds of them, were about four feet tall and each was wrapped in flowers trailing up to a gold colored pot they were planted in. Each time he would pass by a pillar, he would catch the warming aroma given off by the flowers. It was helping to relax him and he could tell it. At the same time, he felt the urgency of getting to his brothers. He knew that he could tell a couple of his brothers, that were aware of his condition, what had happened and find out what his fathers' presentation was about before it started.

The size of the room and the amount of people there made it difficult, but he finally reached one of his brothers.

"Hey bud," Michael said with a 'good to see you' look on his face.

"Michael, good to see you!" he said at about the same time.

Michael approached the oldest brother - - "Hey John, you seen Paul and David?"

Jeff T. Travis

"No, I haven't seen them. There are a lot of people here though. If they are here, it might take you a little while to find them."

"You might try having one of the employees here announce that you're looking for them over the intercom or something - - I mean, I guess they could do that?"

"Good idea John, but I think I'll just look for them a little while longer. If I don't run in to them, I'll try your idea. Quite a place huh?"

"Sure is. Don't know why I'm here, but it is quite a place. Have you seen the paintings on the wall?"

"Wait a minute, you don't know why you're here either?"

"No. Near as I can tell, none of us know what it's going to be about. A few of us have been talking and trying to figure it out and I've asked a couple of the employees here, but they aren't talking."

"You hungry Michael?"

"No I'm stuffed, you?"

"No, me neither. I was going to find you something if you were."

"I appreciate that John, but I'm fine."

"Hey Michael, I'll tell you why I think we're here if you want me to?"

"By all means John, I value your opinion about anything."

"Well, I think we're here to hear someone we know announce their running for city mayor."

Michael thought to himself and smiled as large a smile as he had ever smiled before. "Of course," Michael thought to himself. - - "My father is very well known, liked and respected. Now all the times that his father had discussed politics made perfect sense. He's retired and wants to get into politics. My father, mayor! That's why he didn't know - - his father wanted it to be a surprise. That's why nobody there knew."

"Well thanks John, I think you're absolutely correct! I mean it makes perfect sense. I'm going to walk around a bit a see if I can find Paul and David."

"Okay Michael, I'll see you later. Take a look at the paintings on the wall. I mean, if you like that kind of stuff. It's pretty impressive stuff to me. I've thought and wondered about those very things at one time or another."

"Will do John, see ya bud."

CHAPTER SEVEN – THE PAINTINGS

Michael looked around the room with his mind finally at ease. Smiling all the while, he knew now why he was there. Because he knew this would make his father happy, it made him happy. Here I thought my father was getting old and all this time he was working on this. What a guy! Michael knew his mother would be happy also. She was always telling his father that he needed to find something to occupy a little more of his time, before he got too comfortable in that chair.

While walking, Michael decided he could now focus on finding Lillian. If he ran into Paul and David, that would just be a plus, but he really didn't need to see them right now. He could tell them about his blackout later, so they could document what had happened.

Michael noticed a woman that he thought was Lillian, about a hundred feet away. Her back was turned to him and she was walking in her slow, but certain manner towards the area outside the convention hall where she first called for him.

"I need to follow her and find out what she meant by the comment she made," he thought. "How could she make such a comment without knowing me?" he thought while moving at an accelerated and overtaking pace. Almost within reach now, he turned his head slightly to the right when he caught something out of the corner of his eye. He noticed some paintings through a small void of people, well off in the distance in the corner of the room. "Well those must be the paintings John was talking about." He turned back to focus in on Lillian, but she was gone.

"I can't believe this, she was right in front of me." But again, there were just too many people. It was difficult to navigate through the room, let alone trying to trail a specific person.

Being this close, Michael figured he might as well take a quick peek at the paintings. He knew how John was and when he spoke with him after while, the first thing he'd ask was what he thought about them.

Weaving in and out of people, Michael made his way to the corner of the room. He looked at them and realized that the paintings progressed completely around the room to include what he reasoned to be the stage area. He could tell that the stage was recessed. The corners were not squared off though, they were rounded. As he looked at it, he thought to himself how it made the stage much more interactive for people standing to the side, because they would be able to see as well as anyone in the room.

The entire room was very impressive with its design and features, but Michael focused his attention on the stage and decided to get closer where he could see it better. Weaving in and out of people and pillars, he made his way there.

Instead of the blue flooring he was standing on, it was pure white and elevated several feet. The paintings followed the contours of the rounded walls and stretched across the back of the stage as well. The stage shared the same high ceiling of the rest of the room, with the exception of a large white rectangle, about three to five feet wide, and maybe ten or twelve feet long painted directly in the center of the stage. It was not a light, just a bright, white rectangle running parallel with the stage. The engineer was really quite brilliant, because there were no lights visible to the eye in the stage area either. Michael could only reason that the engineer was able to make use of light from somewhere reflecting from white stage flooring. Glancing that direction, he noticed that other than the white flooring, there was nothing else on the stage. No chairs, no microphone, no curtains, nothing. Except for the microphone, Michael didn't see this as strange, because there were no chairs in the entire room. He recalled his father once did a presentation about sitting back and not taking responsibility for the family. He wondered if somehow the lack of chairs had something to do with that. That his father had the chairs removed to drive a point home.

The Convention

Michael turned his attention back to the paintings. Thinking that he should find a beginning point, he made his way back to where he started. Because of how large the room was and the sheer size of the paintings, he couldn't help but wonder how long this must have taken someone to do, and how much money it must have cost.

The lighting in the convention room, while very pleasant, was still playing tricks on his eyes. As he looked at the paintings, he could tell that the lighting was creating many colors that he couldn't quite identify. At the same time, the colors made for very vivid detail. Again, gazing around the room, it was clear to him that he wouldn't have time to see them all, there appeared to be as many as five hundred, possibly more.

In the corner, was a blank canvas and from that point to the right, the paintings flowed uninterrupted. The clarity and color was amazing and really impressed Michael. Because of the size, he stepped back from the painting a little so he could see it entirely. He wondered if he could get prints on a smaller scale. He knew that the lighting was creating some additional color on the paintings that wouldn't be there when he got them home, but nonetheless, he wanted to try to get prints of what he was seeing. Searching the paintings for the artist's name however drew a blank - - they were not signed. This was clearly an artist who painted for the love of art, not recognition. Michael was sure someone in the convention would be able to connect him to the artist so he wasn't concerned about finding out the name of the artist right now. For the moment, he just wanted to see as many as he could before his father spoke.

While walking around the room, Michael remembered John saying that he had often wondered about the things the artist had painted. As Michael looked, he thought to himself how he agreed with John, he had wondered about these same things as well.

His attention was drawn to the last painting he could see. It was positioned in the corner, to the left of the blank canvas he had started at, he had made his way almost completely around the room. As he walked towards it, he noticed there were several blank canvases prior to it. He pointed his finger at them as he counted and totaled fourteen. As he got closer however, he realized the first of these canvases he thought was blank, was not. It was a work in progress. Standing in front of it now, the painting seemed to take on a life of its own, leaving the canvas as if it were three dimensional, or like he was entering into it. Just like the other features of the room, amazing! He observed it closely trying to determine exactly what it was. It appeared as though vertical lines were coming through on the lower portion of the canvas. Michael liked all the paintings he had time to stop and look at, but felt a true appreciation and bond for this one. It was very hazy and seemed to be extremely distorted. Michael felt that it reminded him of his life. As with the other paintings, it was as though he could reach in, touch, and if he wanted to, remove portions of it. He wouldn't consider touching them though, the artist had put an enormous amount of work into them.

Michael looked away and continued walking until he reached the last painting. Glancing over about ten feet to where he had originally started his way around the room, he wondered how, with those colors, he could have missed it. He could not make out what the artist was doing here though. The canvas was completely covered with yellow, orange and red colors, all three entwined together with nothing else. It seemed to have life, but it didn't have near the life of the other paintings.

With no room above or below the existing paintings, Michael wondered what the artist would choose for the remaining thirteen canvases near the end of the room and the first one in the corner. Many of the paintings were absolutely breathtaking, flawless and beautiful. Others however, while filled with beautiful color, were plain and simply horrifying and quite saddening. Nonetheless, he was sure he wanted prints of many of them to give as gifts to his wife. She had a deep appreciation for art and had excellent decorating skills. She would know exactly where to hang them. He just needed to make sure he got the prints in smaller scale because the paintings were far too large for any house he had ever been in, his salary made sure of that. Michael noticed an employee walking towards him.

"Excuse me, sir?"

"Yes, how can I be of assistance?"

The Convention

"Well, I'm hoping you can tell me the name of the artist here."

"I certainly can. Can you give me just a moment though - - it's not a simple answer? I need to get someone first, and it's really important that I do that now. I mean, I know this is important to you…"

"Please sir," said Michael, "it's fine. You go right ahead. I'm in no hurry. You come back at your convenience. I know with all these people here, you folks have got to be very busy. In fact, I'm kind of sorry now that I didn't think about that. You probably don't have time to stop for a drink of water to quench your thirst."

The employee's eyes lit up while he asked Michael, "Are you thirsty?"

"No, no! Just a figure of speech to describe how busy you must be."

"I assure you sir, I'm fine," he said with a smile. "I really enjoy this job. There is no way I would ever trade it.

Anyway, I'll be back to see you soon about the paintings – okay?"

"That's fine. Please don't rush on my part though."

While standing and looking at the paintings, Michael felt a gentle hand on the back of his shoulder. He turned to see Lillian.

"Hello again Michael."

"Lillian I've been looking for you. I saw you a little while ago, but I couldn't catch up to you. You sure get around pretty fast."

"Yea, I guess I do. It comes with the job around here, but I really wouldn't have it any other way. My father told me once if I ever had a job that I...

"...really liked you'd never work another day in your life," Michael said, completing her sentence.

"That's right, your father told you the same huh? I really do love this and I don't consider it work. I absolutely love it."

"You know, I'm the same way with my job. I wouldn't even consider doing anything else."

"Well after while, I'm going to try and change your mind about that Michael."

"Oh really," he said with a smile. "Best of luck to you Lillian, but I really don't think you have a chance."

"You'd be great, Michael."

"Now wait just a minute Lillian! First the comment you made about me having some special qualities, and now this? Tell me what you mean?"

"Well right now I have to inform everyone that your father is about to speak. Can it wait just a little while?"

Jeff T. Travis

"Come on Lillian, it will only take a moment. It's important to me."

She looked into his eyes and could see just how important this was to him. It reminded her of how she once felt. Needing to know and feel something, but not knowing what it was that needed to be known or felt. It was a nagging void that needed filling. The look in her eyes combined with the expression on her face, insured Michael that she knew exactly how he felt.

"Take my hand Michael," she said while extending her arm with her hand palm side up. "All of life is but a moment Michael. Often times, just a moment of your time will have a life long impact on those affected by it."

"Michael, are you really not aware of how many people you have helped in your lifetime? Do you really not know the positive affect you have had on so many lives and because of that, the positive affect they had on others? Do you really not know that you go to work, not only because you love it, but also to make a living for your family, trying your best to assure they have all they need and some things they want? Do you really not know that you have raised three beautiful children and are instilling the most valuable of values in them? Do you really not know how your wife loves you as much as you love her? Do you really not know that because of things you have done and do, many people love you? Do you really not know how pleased your father is with you? You have a heart of gold Michael - - you love, and you are certainly loved. Michael, I assure you, you have beautiful qualities. All of these things Michael and yet you never feel secure, never feel that you are doing enough, or what you're doing is well enough. Always feeling and believing that there is so much more you can and need to do. One of the most beautiful qualities you have Michael - - is the quality of not believing that you have these qualities," Lillian said while gently lowering her voice and tightening her grasp on his hand ever so slightly firmer.

Michael felt uneasy by what she had just said to him. He tilted his head somewhat while continuing eye contact. "I appreciate that and please don't take this the wrong way, but Lillian, you don't know me! How can you say such things about someone you don't know?"

Jeff T. Travis

"Because I know your father Michael and I know you are here. I know your father wouldn't have you present for this, if these things weren't true. Exactly where you'd be, I don't know for sure, but you wouldn't be here. Trust me Michael. You don't feel comfortable, because you feel a little insecure right now. But you're content with your body and mind and your body and mind has carried out all the good things you have done. I say it again Michael, you have very special qualities."

"Thank you Lillian," he said tearing up through a smile. "I'm not sure I understand what you're saying, but thank you. Sometimes a man just needs to feel good about himself. I guess this was my time."

"No need to thank me Michael," as she brushed her hair off of her left shoulder and allowed it to fall across her back exposing her neck and shoulder. "You're a very intelligent man. It will all make sense to you."

As she brushed her hair off her shoulder, Michael spotted something very familiar to him.

"Lillian?"

"Yes Michael, what is it?"

"Where did you get that necklace?" he said with an expression of concern.

Lillian reached and grasped the necklace with her right hand and turned her eye to Michael.

"Aged And Aging. You know Mrs. Corning!? That necklace is identical to hers, isn't it? Is she okay? Where is she?"

"Yes, I do. Yes Michael, it is. I assure you she is fine and she's close."

"Well, where is she? I really need to explain something to her."

"Okay, I promise I'll bring her to you very soon."

"You know Michael, Mrs. Corning speaks of the 'AAA' as Aged And Aging. It's very true and I like that, but I prefer Angels All Around."

"Angels All Around huh? You know, I've had some pretty close calls in my time. I've often wondered if I had a guardian angel. I remember one time walking down the street, if I hadn't stopped to buy a newspaper on that corner, a car that jumped the sidewalk would have hit me, I'm certain of it."

"Michael, I want you to listen to me."

The lighting in the room suddenly changed. The paintings on the walls were only barely visible now. A white fog began pouring from the stage area and bottom of the paintings and was filling up vacant floor space to about two feet high. Everyone present became very still.

"Now that's kind of weird Lillian."

"Shhh. Stay right here beside me Michael and keep your eyes on the front of the room," Lillian said in a whisper.

"Your father is ready to speak Michael. Isn't this exciting and dramatic," she said continuing with a whisper.

"Yea Man, talk about an entrance. This is going to be one for the books. I wish Lynn and the boys were here to see this."

"Shhh."

"Well quit talking to me and I won't feel obligated to answer," he said jokingly.

"Okay, now shhh."

Michael continued chuckling, but it was a silent chuckle.

The center stage area continued to light up. Light was dropping slowly downward from the white rectangle painted on the ceiling above the stage until it reached the floor. Soon, the rectangle was so bright it was difficult to see through it to the paintings behind it. It resembled driving into a whiteout condition from snow, so much snow that you can't see the snow. This light was so bright that you couldn't see the light, it was simply white. Michael was looking almost directly ahead. He shifted his body so he could get a look behind the light. From that angle, he could see that only the face of the light was white. The remaining portion of the rectangle, while obviously light, was a much clearer light, it almost resembled water that was capturing light. It was lighter than all the area outside the rectangle, but nothing compared to the face of the light. He shifted his body back and while looking at the face of the light, could make out two figures. Because of the lighting, the figures appeared to blend almost perfectly with the light. Michael could see that the colors from the paintings on the stage were reflecting onto the figures as well and created a kind of rainbow color effect.

"Lillian this can't be right, this lighting desperately needs fixed, it's terrible – I can't even make out their bodies, let alone their faces. Can you call someone to fix this? He'll be the laughing stock if this continues."

"No Michael, he won't. Trust me, everything is fine. This is exactly what is supposed to happen."

The Convention

He could tell by her smile that she was perfectly fine with it; she knew exactly what was going on.

"Oh I get it! This is part of the intro - - an attention getter. Or what did you call it, a mood setter?" as he looked and pointed towards the door they had entered through. Looking at the doorway, he could see that it resembled the rectangle light that was now on the stage. He turned his head back towards the stage as he heard a very commanding, yet at the same time, kind and gentle voice.

CHAPTER EIGHT - MICHAEL'S FATHER SPEAKS

"First My children, I welcome you."

"I am your Father, I am the Father, I am the Sovereign One, I am truly the Lord thy God! I Am!"

"You are My children and I love you. I am everything that is beautiful and nothing that is not beautiful. Even to your oldest day I am He. I am the One who has made you and I am the One who will sustain, carry, comfort and rescue you. Know now My children that even before you were born, I knew you and placed much value on you."

"Indeed, even the very hairs on your head are numbered, known unto Me and are held precious to Me."

The Convention

"Know now My children that truly you are with Me."

There was a pause and instantly, Michael and everyone else in the room fell to their knees as if their legs had lost any and all strength to support them. At the same time, Michael realized that the language that had been spoken was foreign to him and he didn't speak any other language. He knew he could understand every word being said though and he could tell that everyone else in the room could too.

"Oh my God!" Michael said as he looked towards Lillian. As he did, he realized she was also turning to look at him. He looked into her eyes. She was smiling, while he had a terrified look on his face. She said nothing, yet he could hear her voice. The voice started as Lillian, but suddenly changed and became Lilly Corning. At the same time, her appearance turned to Mrs. Corning, but remained only for a moment and then returned as it had been. "I don't understand! What's going on here Lillian?" Michael said taking a step back.

Lillian took a small step in his direction.

"Stay right there!" he said while raising his right hand with his palm towards her.

"Please don't be frightened Michael," as she stopped. "The Father has instructed each of us to explain something to you at this very moment."

Michael looked around the room and could see that each and every person there was speaking with an employee. He put his hands over his eyes and shook his head back and forth. "This has something to do with my blackouts, this can't be right."

"Michael, I was instructed to stay near you during the tragedy."

"Tragedy - - what tragedy?"

"Look into my eyes Michael," she said as he removed his hands from his face. "Look deeply Michael and see what the Father now chooses for you to remember."

The Convention

Michael looked deep into her eyes and could see the tragedy she was referring to. Now the painting that was distorted and hazy made perfect sense, as he looked toward the painting which mysteriously was completed now. Michael could see the detail in the once distorted and hazy painting very vividly, but it was far too painful for him to look at. He pulled his eyes away and could see the painting to the right had also taken form. It was people being held in the palm of one giant hand with the other giant hand, palm down, being held over the top of the ground. Michael stood there staring with tears flowing down his cheeks. He was in total shock as to what he was seeing.

"No! This can't be true!" Michael said with certainty and disbelief.

"Yes Michael. I'm very sorry, it is true. There was no blackout this day Michael and the stress that brought the blackouts about is gone forever. Because I had followed your family so long, I knew that you wouldn't let me help you directly Michael, so I had to help you by having you help me. I knew that such a kind and giving man would not leave a person in need, no matter the circumstances Michael. You are the man you have always aspired to be like. Angels All Around Michael, Angels All Around. Don't be frightened Michael, turn and listen to your Father."

"I have made promises to you, many promises. I have given you things, many things. And yet there is much more I hold to give you. Gifts greater than your very imagination. Of what I have already given to you, faith, hope and love are the most valuable. Any of My children who have love, by My grace, have Me. Any of My children who do not have love, do not have Me."

"I say these initial things to you because I am love! I am the purest love. And of all the things I have already given to you, the greatest and most precious, is love."

"Yes, I have given you faith, I have given you hope and I have given you love. I also have given you freewill. Yet, I did not give you freewill to direct your faith, hope and love without direction. I ordered unto you through the child Moses, My commandments and I also provided you with My word. My word given to you through Me and the Son. The

Son with whom I am most pleased and has earned his place here to My right."

"My word scribed to teach you and placed in the form of a book, so that you may have faith - - faith to compliment your hope, hope to compliment your love, and love to compliment your faith. You were told to remain strong in your faith to Me and in doing so, My words and Me would remain strong in you."

"Be ye not deceived, it is by virtue of My grace I have given you the opportunity for eternal life. Your works alone will not gain you a place in My kingdom. This I told you so that you would not go astray and so you would not be deceived."

"I tell you now in this moment, that one of My children strong in faith, hope and love, is indeed loved by Me and carries the weight of one million, million sparrows in My eyes."

"Each of you have seen the documents on the walls that you discuss, one to the other, as paintings. As it was written, any and all questions for which you seek answers, those answers will be revealed to you. While one of you sees the fifth document as one question you carry, 10,000 may see the fifth document as completely different. The document you review reveals answers to those questions you have carried. Many others may carry the same question and as such, many may see the fifth document as being the same document."

"Know this My children, the documents you see before you are as they were, cannot be changed, and need no interpretation. They are now as they were then. They are now as they will be with the rise of each morning sun. They are of Me and as such, they are pure truth. If you seek an answer, look to the documents and that truth will be revealed to you. Enter that document and I am there."

"Just as I am the Alpha and the Omega, the first and last documents are the Alpha and Omega, the beginning and the end. All will see these first and last documents in the same manner and in the same position, because they are the beginning and the end. Without any one of these, there is no between. Just as the beginning and the end are of Me, so to are all those of the middle. The beginning and the end are today as they were yesterday and will be with the rise of each morning sun."

"This I tell you is the very foundation of all I have made from that day to this and this day to that. All things are created to provide for balance. Balance through freewill. Freewill will bring forth bad, freewill will bring forth good. And freewill will bring forth those things that are neither bad nor good, but are necessary for balance of all things. And all things are designed to balance on their own - - just as electricity escapes the good earth into the heavens during lightening storms."

"Just as it is with balance of electricity, it is with all things known and unknown to the people of the good earth. Indeed, it is true of all things except Me. For all who have come before you, and you, and all who will come after you, combining your numbers, your wisdom, your faith, your hope and your love - - you will at that last moment, even combined, remain short by one measure of all that is good as compared against Me."

"For all of the population from that day to this, and from this day to that, all will make their choices in determining the balance with their freewill - - choosing how they will apply their faith, their hope, and their love."

"Yet, the scale cannot tip from one side to the other. For just as there is one on the left who would use his freewill to do harm, there is one on the right who stands upright before Me."

"And just as there are 10,000 who stand upright in the eyes of the Lord, there is one who leads 9,999 out of the light. But just as 9,999 can be lead out of the light, one can carry far greater weight in the eyes of the Lord than that of the 10,000 as measured by their faith, hope and love. It is a perfect balance."

"My children, in My eyes you stand very tall upon your knees. Rise and fear not now. Behold My children, those who would choose to bring fear, sorrow and harm upon you."

Instantly, there were nineteen men standing in the center of the room. Michael couldn't tell exactly what it was, but it looked as though there was a shield of glass completely surrounding them, a shield of glass that resembled a flowing liquid much like the light behind the white light.

"Hear Me now."

"I AM!

"And just as I AM, the Son is.

"And just as the Son is, the Son is of Me.

"And just as the Son is, and the Son is of Me, Angels are.

"And just as Angels are, Angels are Holy Spirits, Holy Spirits of the Son.

"And just as Angels are, and Angels are Holy Spirits of the Son, Angels are of Me.

"And none come to Me, but thru the Son, guided here by My Holy Spirit, My Angels."

"Be ye not deceived. Those were the words given to you. Instead you nineteen chose to place the freewill of your faith, hope and love in those who would take My word and contort it, and deceive you with their sharpened tongues."

"You allowed these few, these few who would not martyr themselves to deceive you. And you then either chose to be martyred, or were chosen for martyrdom. Because you allowed yourself to be deceived against the word, it matters not in this house that you were chosen to be martyred with or without your knowledge."

"In so doing, you and those you chose to follow have brought much shame to a good flock.

"In doing so, you have brought life to those whom you would have dead, and death to those whom you sought to bring eternal life."

"Just as it is I, and I alone who brings life, it is I, and I alone who brings death. Hear me now. There is a time for peace, just as there is a time for war. Only that war which is justified and sanctified through Me is of the time. Yours was not justified! Yours was not sanctified! Yours was not of the time!"

"Behold My children. Behold what these nineteen and those they follow have chosen with their freewill."

Again there was a pause and the painting that had been hazy and distorted and then was mysteriously finished, began to expand simultaneously from the top, bottom and sides. It continued to expand until all portions of the room were occupied by it. The floor, walls, ceiling and the pillars and flowers. Everything was completely covered by the painting. When it finished, all the people in the room were in the painting, and standing within the horror and devastation. Everywhere Michael looked was destruction. The people, who they were now among, were running away covered in dust and debris, gasping for air. At times, the people were running directly through them while they stood there. The people were crying and in absolute disbelief as to what was happening. Still others were digging into the rubble and wreckage trying to help those in need.

Michael looked over to his left viewing the devastation. He could tell that what he was seeing, though the colors were connected, were part of a separate event. He was looking into the middle of a field with wreckage all around. There were bodies in and around the wreckage and people running towards it. Other people who were already there were looking for survivors, digging through the wreckage with their bare hands. The sight became far too much for some to bear and they were putting their hands over their eyes, obviously crying.

Looking to his right, he could see the Pentagon. The wall of the building had been caved in and people were running in and out even while it was ablaze desperately trying to get people out of the building. He could see senior government officials tending to those in need as well. In this, there was clearly no separation in the people, everyone was helping frantically and equally.

"Enough! My heart weeps for you nineteen. My heart weeps for you far more than you, even combined, now weep for yourselves."

And as quick as those words were completed, the room returned as it was, the painting was back in place and the nineteen men were on their knees with their heads bowed to the floor.

"Hear Me My good flock. As the document reveals, it was not the work of these nineteen who brought down the number 93 aircraft. Rather it was forty of you who would not be deceived by four of these nineteen on that aircraft, who with sharpened tongues told you no harm would come. Truly your faith is strong and the love shown is worthy of many blessings."

"Your not being deceived, saved much more loss than you shall ever know. For unto Me was known the intended destination of the aircraft. It was not the number 93 aircraft that placed a crater upon the earth."

"Hear Me now. Each of you were accompanied by Angels I had sent in advance to insure that you would experience no suffering. It was I who placed the crater, when My right hand hit upon the earth ahead of the impact, only a moment before, and collected your very souls insuring no suffering."

"Hear Me My good flock. As the document reveals, it was not the number 77 aircraft that produced the hole in the side of your pentagon. Rather it was My hand that opened the wall ahead of the impact, only by a moment before, to collect your very souls, along with the souls present in the building, insuring no suffering."

"Where you call for me, so shall I be there. Till the earth and I am there, ripple the water and My robe distorts, touch the air and you shall find Me. During that time just before the moment, your love for one another was self evident. Consoling the frightened around you and praying for those you feared you might be leaving behind. Truly I tell you, each of you were accompanied by Angels I had sent in advance to insure that you would experience no suffering. My precious children, your prayers were heard even before you finished. Heard and answered as promised by My grace."

The Convention

"Hear Me My good flock. As the document reveals, it was not the work of these nineteen that brought down your twin towers with the numbers 11 and 175 aircrafts. Rather it was My right hand, necessarily so, that forced the towers straight down to the earth."

"Hear Me now My children. While several thousand of you have joined Me here on this, your eleventh day of the ninth month, seven times your amount are left to continue their good work. And while you were within the confines of the towers, you were not alone."

"Each of you were accompanied by Angels I had sent in advance to insure that you would experience no suffering."

"The time the towers were to be forced to the earth was known unto Me, and Me alone. You who are with Me this day, are with Me because the moment the towers were to fall, was to happen one moment before you could have possibly escaped the towers."

"Holding My hand back until another moment, far more would have been killed, as many more would have been in reach of and entered the towers to help, than would have escaped the towers. Had I forced the towers any sooner, seven times your amount would not be left to continue the good work I have planned for them."

"Truly I tell you, not one of you experienced any pain. For before My right hand forced the towers straight down to the earth, My left and merciful hand dug deep into the earth on the underneath of the towers and lifted up and through, collecting your very souls like wind collecting leaves from the trees."

"Even those of you who leapt from the towers did so through Me. Truly I tell you, I will never give you more than you can handle. I watched over each of you carefully. When I saw that suffering was near, I collected your souls just as the others. Indeed, it was through your faith that you are here today as it was I and I alone who called you through the windows and into My left hand where your very souls were caught and held close to My heart. Because of your faith, you are truly loved."

"And what greater love than that, where one of My children willingly gives his life for another, another he knows not. You have shown the purity of love. Truly I tell you that such love is pure in heart, and blessed are the pure in heart in the eyes of the Lord."

Michael suddenly realized he was being elevated from the floor. He had a look of both amazement and fear on his face while remaining suspended some ten feet above the floor. Michael looked around for a moment and could see his brother firefighters and other people he did not recognize suspended with him. He noticed that anyone who had not been elevated, bowed their heads to the floor.

"Blessed are the pure in heart. Behold My blessed children!"

Michael looked and became overwhelmed with emotion, just as all those who were suspended did. He had never seen such a kind and beautiful sight. Far beyond description, Michael had only one thought repeating through his mind - - love, pure love. Everyone who was suspended bore the same awestruck expression and most, including Michael, were crying tears of overwhelming joy and love. Michael and his brothers, along with the others, were then lowered gently back to the floor.

"You nineteen are no longer worthy of sharing this space with the good flock. You are returned to your encasement where you shall await your judgment. Where soon you will come to realize My displeasure. Where soon you will know that I am the Lord. Where soon, you will know!" With a subtle wave of the hand, the nineteen men vanished.

"Hear Me now My children."

"Because they are lacking so in their faith, hope and love in that they allowed themselves to be deceived. Because they placed their faith in the tongue of those who twisted a good word. Because they placed their hope in the lips of those who brought shame to a good and spiritual flock. Because they placed their precious love in the very hands of those who dare to subscribe to a war not justified and sanctified through Me, who live only to bring about fear of them, when I am the only one to be feared! And because they made it their life's work to bring death, when I and only I bring death, their judgment falls upon them."

"Just as you thousands were approached and pleaded with to ask for forgiveness before your time was upon you, they were approached and requested not to continue with this thing they had conspired to do. They were approached during their wake and they were approached during their sleep."

"It was asked of them, no fewer than seven times each, with the first of the requests coming long before this day and the last of these requests coming this day, not to do as they had conspired to do. They were asked through a child's face, a woman's tears, and a man's heart. Each time, the requests were dismissed.

"The very children, women and men whom they denied, were those I had sent in advance in an attempt to reach them, indeed to prevent their actions, so they might turn against the sharp tongues of those they used their freewill to follow. Through their freewill and because they were deceived, they chose to ignore the pleas of My blessed children."

"Know this, I am against the charm with which their leaders deceive My people to perform their murderous actions. Know that I will tear My precious children from their arms when they come to Me through the Son. Indeed, I will rescue them and hold them close to my heart."

"I will tear off the masks of their leaders exposing them to all, and I will save My people from their murderous hands. They will no longer fall victim to their sharp tongues and deceitful lips. Then they shall come to know."

"I will pull together the people of the nations of the good earth and they will be justified and sanctified in their war against them and their leaders. Their deceiving leaders, and all those who will follow them will be at war for the remaining moments of their lives."

"When all the nations have come together, their deceiving leaders and all those who follow them will have surely lost. They will cower and hide in the dredges and caves of the earth where I will starve them and plague them with disease. Then they shall come to know!"

"I will bring up their own people against them when their deceiving masks are removed, and their own people will hunt them down giving them no rest, nor food, nor water, nor shelter and they will lend them their ear no more."

"Hear Me now. Just as any one of you good flock gathered here today weighs more in My eyes than 1 million, million sparrows, so too, does 1 thousand of those nineteen, and all those they used their freewill to follow, weigh less than that of a single mustard seed in My eyes."

"Truly I say to you, that all of the good flock present here today will be forever remembered by My children remaining behind and through the document of life I have already scribed. As surely as they shall be forgotten, you shall be remembered. Those nineteen, and their leaders, will be stricken from record and forgotten. True martyrdom is achieved by love, the love expressed by all of you here this moment."

"By that, those nineteen are not worthy of this place and their judgment falls upon them like a thief in the night. Like a thief in the night because they did not seek forgiveness for their sins before their moment came unto them."

"Because of this, they may look upon the document of life, but will not see their reflection scribed there. And no reflection, yields no entry into My kingdom."

"It is not, however, because their reflection is not scribed, it is because they cannot stand upright in front of the document of life."

"Because they cannot stand upright in the document of life, and because their freewill brought about much destruction, these nineteen missed the measure by 99 percent of their faith, hope and love, failing to keep My commandments and My word close to their heart."

"Because of this, all their goodness combined is outbalanced by the weight of a single mustard seed."

"Soon - - the nineteen will know that I Am!"

"Soon - - the nineteen and those who lead them will know that I am the Lord."

"Soon - - Vengeance will be Mine! My heart will weep even more than they will weep for themselves, but vengeance will be Mine!"

"Hear Me now My children. I am today as I am yesterday. I am tomorrow as I am today. From that moment to this, and from this moment to that, I am unchanging. I am the Alpha, I am the Omega. I am the beginning and I am the end. Just as I am the beginning and just as I am the end, I am the center, the very center of all things. Things as they are, things as they were, and things as they shall be. I AM!"

"The documents you see as unfinished are not unfinished, only unrevealed unto you. Unrevealed because the events they are to stand as testimony to have yet to come. This document you see as light that descends around Me from the very heavens, this is the document of life. Only those souls scribed by My hand may see it and must stand upright to look upon it - - stand upright in the eyes of thy God. And those that see it, while looking upon it, may approach. And those who see it, approach it and stand upright before it, may certainly pass through it and enter My kingdom. There remains much I want to give to you, and all awaits those who enter. All who exceed the great balance by their good works and their faith, hope and love may enter through My grace. All of you who remain here this very moment, have been scribed into the document of life and you are welcome."

"Again I say to you, none of you entered even into this place alone. The one who brought you unto Me, through the Son, will as Me, assist you for and through Me.

The Convention

Welcome My children, welcome. My love and grace will follow you with whichever decision you make. I love you now as I have always loved you, and will always love you, even until the end - - and beyond the end. You are Mine and My blessings befall you."

    The light lifted and He was gone.

CHAPTER NINE – THE DECISION

"Michael. Are you okay Michael?" Lillian said softly with her hand gently touching his shoulder.

Michael, looking at Lillian, began crying, holding his hands over his face as if he were embarrassed. "So that's it, I'm dead? - - What's going to happen to my wife and children? - - What about my mother and father? What about my other brothers at the fire station?"

"Listen to yourself Michael. Here you are - - 'dead!' You come to the realization and what is the first thing you wonder about... not yourself, but your family and friends. You have reacted just as I knew you would Michael. Yes, you are such a good man."

The Convention

"You mean were, don't you!? Don't you mean were, Lillian!?"

"No Michael, the wording I use is quite accurate. You think you have died, but in reality, you have only just begun to live. Listen to me Michael. Do you understand what has happened today Michael? I mean really understand?"

"I guess I must not Lillian! God just finished speaking to me and I thought he was speaking to me because I was dead. You say I'm not dead, that I've only just begun to live. If I am here, then I am not there. If I'm not there, I can't be with my wife and children. I'm telling you now Lillian, if I can't be with my wife and children, I am dead! Do you hear me Lillian, dead!"

"Listen to me Michael."

"No Lillian, not if you're going to talk in puzzles. I can't take that right now Lillian - - I just can't."

"Michael, a little while ago I told you I was going to try to get you to change jobs. Do you remember what you said to me? Look at me Michael. Please." she said while Michael was looking to the floor with his hands covering his face. "You smiled at me and said, 'Best of luck to you Lillian, but I really don't think you have a chance'."

"Yea, so,?" while raising his head to make eye contact with her.

"So your freewill doesn't end with your life on earth Michael. You have the choice to enter into the document of life, or to proudly wear a necklace identical to this one."

"The necklace your father gave you when you were twenty four?"

"Yes Michael. I died on the operating table that day - - the day my father gave me this necklace."

"So it was you that my mother and father were speaking about that day? I'm confused Lillian."

"Yes Michael, it was. Let me explain."

The Convention

"Michael, when you saw me as Lilly Corning in that stairwell, you saw me as I needed you to see me, so I could make sure you stayed with me. I have loved your family so long, I wanted to make sure I did everything I could to make sure you were going to have the very best in your after life. That is why I wanted you to ask for forgiveness, and ask for it in the name of the Son, Jesus Christ. I knew something was going to happen and I knew I couldn't change it, but I also knew that would be my last opportunity to protect you. In the stairwell when I told you I was sharing in your forgiveness, I was Michael. You said it was air and you were somewhat correct, but it wasn't just air, it was the Father's hand collecting your soul at His moment, His exact moment. That was your moment Michael. In the middle of your sentence, that was your moment. Just as you had your moment, I did in fact, as you say 'die', many years prior and the day I died, my father did give me this necklace. I looked then exactly as you see me now. When I say my father gave me this necklace though, I mean my FATHER."

"Remove my scarf from your hand Michael."

"Scarf? I had forgotten that I even had it on my hand," Michael said as he removed it and handed it to Lillian.

"Turn your hand over and look. Look at the gaping wound on your hand Michael!"

Turning his hand over to where he had cut himself, he looked to find nothing. No wound, no scar, no nothing. His eyes were wide open and she now had his complete attention.

"All of your scars are healed Michael, including the burn scar on your right arm. The day I died, God accepted me Michael. He accepted me and healed my wounds and removed my scars. As I told you in the stairwell, no doctor on earth could have healed my wounds. And a little child who had brought me to this place, just as I brought you here, convinced me to do what I do now. When I looked into the document of my life, I saw what your father and mother had tried to do for me, and I saw the note they had sent for me. It so touched me, that I made it my point to look after all of you from that day forward."

"You've been looking over my family?"

"Yes Michael, me and others."

"Others? Others like who?"

Lillian glanced to the side ever so slightly and nudged her eyes for Michael to look that direction.

"Willie? Is that you Willie?"

"Sure is Michael, good to see you."

"Well I often wondered who helped who more on that little trip. How did you protect me? I always felt something."

"Well actually Michael, your father did the protecting that day. You see, I was there, meaning I hadn't come here yet. Lillian placed me on that interstate and worked very hard to do it."

"How did you and Lillian know each other?"

"We had been married."

"Now wait a minute, I remember you saying your wife's name was Brenda, no, Barbara. I remember that very well."

"Yes I did, you're correct. Barbara was my second wife. Lillian here was my first wife. We didn't have much time together, but the time we had, helping those villagers was wonderful. Michael, Lillian worked hard to get me to want to travel that far to see my daughter and just as hard for my daughter to want me to come and visit her. Lillian used me because she knew your father would do what he did. And by doing what your father did, he protected you and your mother that day. At the same time, she managed to heal the relationship between me and my daughter by getting us to spend some quality time together. So you see, had your father not turned the station wagon around to help me that day, the vehicle would have been involved in the crash a few miles ahead of where you were at the time and your family would have ended up under the semi you saw still on its side when you went back through. So you see,

Lillian didn't change what was to happen, your father did by deciding to be such a very good man. I'll tell you, your father is a very intelligent man as well. The note he left me in my bag… he really understands people."

"I knew he had left you a note, but I never knew what it said," Michael said with a grin.

Willie smiled and held out his hand holding a paper napkin and unfolding it while extending the note towards Michael. Michael could see that it was his fathers' handwriting even before Willie handed him the note.

Dear Mr. Hanover,

I want to thank you for sharing so many beautiful stories with us today. If you don't mind, I would appreciate your doing something for me.

You are going to want to help your daughter get through this difficult time and I understand that. I have a feeling however, that your daughter is going to want to help you get through it. I think you will help your daughter much more if you allow her to help you. Based on everything we talked about, I believe it will make her a much stronger person.

You're already strong. Show your strength by pretending to be a little weak, just for a while.

p.s. I know a good and reliable man when I meet one. If you want a job after spending some time with your daughter, please give me a call. I have a friend with a business and you would be a true blessing for him.

God Bless and keep you Mr. Hanover,

James

"There's a lot of wisdom in that little note Michael. It allowed me to become closer to my daughter than I had been in years. I knew we lived miles apart, but I hadn't realized we had grown so far apart. You see, by pretending to be weak for a while, my daughter came to my rescue. After she came to my rescue, I slowly regained my strength. I could see it in her eyes each day Michael, she loved caring for me. Every day that I got stronger, the strength in her eyes became more apparent. No doubt about it, that little note did a whole lot of good for me and my daughter. I can truly say it is one of the things that helped me with my decision."

"What decision is that Willie?" asked Michael.

Lillian looked at Michael with the same look Mrs. Corning had given him earlier in the stairwell.

"Michael, you need to decide if you want to enter into the kingdom now, or stay behind and continue your good works helping others and enter the Kingdom at a another time."

"Helping others, as in being an Angel?"

"Yes Michael, that's right."

"Would this mean that I could visit my wife and kids, my other family members and my brothers?"

"Yes it does Michael, no question about it, as long as you remain within the rules."

"Well, what are the rules?"

"Will you do me a favor before I tell you Michael?"

"Of course I will Lillian. I owe you so much more than I could ever repay. What can I do for you?"

"I want you to stand here Michael, stand here and look to the document of life. When it descends, I want you to read it and pass through it"

"Lillian!"

"Listen to me Michael. I want you to do what I do, with all my heart Michael. But I would be very selfish if I convinced you to do this without your first seeing what our good Lord has prepared for you. Michael it is so incredibly beautiful, beyond description. I just want you to see for yourself what God has prepared for you before you make any decision Michael."

"Now once there, if you decide that you want to return to this place, all you need to do is turn around with the thought of returning here in your mind. At that very instant Michael, you will be returned to this very place. I will hear your desire to return here and will be standing here when you return, I absolutely promise you that."

"What about my wife and children Lillian?" he said with deep concern.

"Willie and I will continue to watch over everyone you hold dear, I promise you that as well."

Michael looked at Lillian and she could see the continued apprehension in his eyes.

"Listen to me Michael, you have absolutely nothing to fear. I promise you Michael, you have only more love and beauty than you can imagine awaiting you beyond the document."

Michael looked deep into her eyes and could see the honesty of his mother's eyes when he was a child and she would console him. Michael was then given all the strength he needed. He looked to the document and it descended from the heavens. He took a step forward standing with his face nearly touching the light as it projected down. He took one last glance over his shoulder at Willie and then Lillian and reached out his hand and arm into the document.

He watched while the portion of his turnout gear, that was inside the light, disappeared and his hand and arm turned white, while silver flakes floated aimlessly around it as he moved his fingers and rotated his hand. Looking directly ahead, he could see his name along with every major point of his life listed below it. At the very bottom was written:

The Convention

"Come to Me child Michael, see what your God has prepared for you. I love you more than you can even imagine is possible. All awaits you by My grace and now you will know not only that I AM, but that you are of Me. Come child, come."

A feeling of overwhelming peace and tranquility came over Michael. He knew immediately that everything was going to be fine. He turned to Lillian and smiled, giving her a look of unlimited thanks. She was standing beside Willie holding her necklace between the fingers of her right hand and nodding her head, indicating to Michael that everything would be fine.

"I love you Michael, I love you." she whispered while giving Michael a wink and a tear.

Michael returned the wink to Lillian, "I love you too, Lillian."

As he watched Lillian place her hands to her face interlocking her fingers, he directed his attention back to the document. With his eyes wide open, he took one final step,

Jeff T. Travis

disappeared and slowly ascended into the heavens with the document.

<u>The Beginning.</u>

This book is dedicated to the following:

1) Family members and friends of the souls of the September 11th attacks who now watch over and protect you. It's true, it's true!

2) The memory of John L. Hancock of Wichita Falls, Texas. A very good friend, spiritual mentor and pilot of so much more than airplanes. I'll never forget the things he was kind enough to share with me and the positive impact he had on my life.

3) AAA

A note from the Author:

You have been given freewill. Freewill along with faith, hope and love. The impact you have on the balance is ever present and has lifelong implications when it is used, and not used. Keep the Word and the Commandments dear to your heart and know that when you do good, that good is multiplied and multiplied and multiplied. May God Bless and keep you.

About The Author

Husband and father of three, Jeff lives in Ohio. While he has written numerous "book style" work related items and a published novelty book, this is his first attempt at an actual book, which is part one of three.

Printed in the United Kingdom
by Lightning Source UK Ltd.
120887UK00001B/106-120